This Book
Belongs To

....

....

RUPERT

C L A S S I C ™

A Collection of Favourite Stories

with original illustrations by
Alfred E. Bestall

EGMONT

EGMONT
We bring stories to life

First published in Great Britain 2007
by Egmont UK Limited
239 Kensington High Street, London W8 6SA
Edited by Sharika Sharma
Designed by Catherine Ellis

EXPRESS NEWSPAPERS

ISBN 978 1 4052 3074 2
1 3 5 7 9 10 8 6 4 2
Printed in Singapore

CONTENTS

EDITOR'S NOTE

Rupert Bear is one of the most famous and enduring characters in children's literature.

Born in 1892, Alfred Edmeades Bestall is best known worldwide for his stories about Rupert. He started illustrating and writing the Rupert Bear stories for the *Daily Express* in 1935. His finest artwork and the best, and most popular, stories have been reproduced in this collection, which includes 'Rupert and Raggety' and 'Rupert and Jack Frost'.

In this collection, the stories have been ordered by the seasons, in keeping with the style of the annuals. Each season is separated by some of Bestall's most lavishly illustrated endpapers, including 'Frog Chorus' from the 1958 annual which inspired Paul McCartney's song 'We All Stand Together' and the animated film, *Rupert and the Frog Song.*

The endpapers that separate the stories have been chosen for their superb illustrations that evoke the comfort of Nutwood as well as the allure of a dreamlike and evocative other world. Rather than being from the same year as the story they precede, the endpapers continue the seasonal progression of this collection, closing with a winter fantasy, 'Night – Santa Claus', from the 1951 annual.

Egmont would like to pay special thanks to Phil Toze for sharing his knowledge in the development of this book, and to Caroline Bott for her kind permission to reproduce previously unpublished cover sketches by her 'Uncle Fred'. These appear in their entirety in the 'Sketchbook' section on pages xiv–xvii.

Rupert's world is timeless. This unique collection will capture the imagination of a new generation.

FOREWORD

Gyles Brandreth is an author, broadcaster, former MP and Lord Commissioner of the Treasury, who, with his wife Michèle Brown, founded the award-winning Teddy Bear Museum, now at the Polka Theatre in Wimbledon, and curated the National Portrait Gallery's exhibition of twentieth-century children's authors.

Welcome to the wonderful world of Rupert Bear. As far as I am concerned he is, as Ben Jonson said of William Shakespeare, 'not of an age, but for all time!' Rupert is one of the great immortal characters of children's literature. As Shakespeare said of Cleopatra, 'age cannot wither' him, nor 'custom stale' his 'infinite variety'. In my book, Rupert is as fresh and endearing today as he was when he first sprang to life almost ninety years ago.

This anthology contains pure gold: eight of the very best – most exciting, most evocative and most compelling – of Rupert's adventures, created between 1944 and 1969 by the great Alfred Bestall (1892–1986), the most celebrated of all the illustrators of Rupert.

Bestall was an artist touched with genius. He illustrated stories by A. A. Milne and Enid Blyton among others, and he drew for magazines such as *Punch* and *Tatler* in their heyday, but it is for his work with Rupert that he will be remembered. Rupert brought out the best in Bestall. From 1935, for almost half a century, Alfred Bestall brought Nutwood to life with matchless imaginative flair and a unique quality of draughtsmanship. He brought his genius to the world of Rupert – and, as his god-daughter Caroline Bott will tell you in her Introduction, his love of origami, too. He invented several of the stories' most engaging characters – including Tigerlily and the Old Professor. But Bestall did not create Rupert. That distinction belongs to Mary Tourtel.

Mary Tourtel (née Caldwell, 1874–1948) was a remarkable individual, a woman of courage and spirit and a pioneer aviatrix, among other things. She came from an artistic family and won a range of awards at art school before going on to work as an illustrator, specialising in animal pictures. In 1920, her husband, Herbert Tourtel, a part-time poet and full-time newspaper executive at the *Daily Express*, knowing that his editor was looking for a children's character to compete with those being created for other newspapers, suggested that his wife might be able to come up with something suitable. She did. Rupert, in a story entitled 'Little Lost Bear', made his very first appearance in the *Daily Express* on Monday 8 November, 1920. He never looked back.

Mary Tourtel (with occasional verses contributed by her poet husband) wrote and illustrated Rupert for fifteen years, until 1935, when failing eyesight forced her to retire and Alfred Bestall took over at the drawing board.

Mary Tourtel is one of the unsung heroines of children's literature. Alfred Bestall is one of the greatest illustrators of all time. Tourtel invented a truly original hero – half-boy, half-bear, wholly Rupert – whose charm and understated charisma have stood the test of time. But, together, Tourtel and Bestall did more than create a series of memorable adventures for a single star character: between them they conjured up a complete imaginative world. It is not the world as it is: it is the world as I would love it to be!

Dear reader, this book is your passport to Nutwood. You are off on a wonderful journey. Enjoy.

INTRODUCTION

by Caroline Bott, god-daughter of Alfred Bestall

Alfred Bestall was very fond of children. Although he never married and didn't have children of his own, he said he felt as if he had thousands of them. He was a relative and my godfather but I did not actually meet him until I was five years old. I had spent the War years with my mother and brother in Australia and he had sent out my first Rupert Annual in 1944.

When we came 'home' we were living at first with my grandparents in Devon and he came to see us. It was pouring with rain one day and we were sitting in a bus shelter in Torrington waiting for a bus to take us home. To pass the time 'Uncle Fred' made paper models (origami) and flew them across the bus shelter. The following year (1946) he introduced an origami page (how to make a paper bird) into the Rupert Annual. If you look carefully, you will often find an origami figure in his covers or endpapers (the pictures inside the hard cover). He also put his initials and my brother's and mine on the luggage in the title page of the story *Rupert and 'Rastus*.

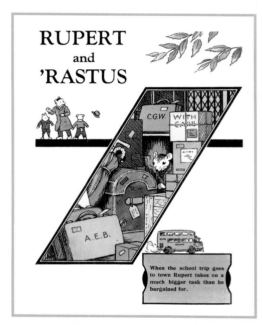

The title page of *Rupert and 'Rastus*

For much of his life Alfred lived in Surbiton, Surrey, and there is now a blue plaque on his house in Cranes Park. Before he began writing and illustrating the Rupert stories in 1935, he worked as a freelance artist. He contributed work to *Punch*, *Tatler*, *Eve* and many other periodicals of the day. In 1926 he illustrated an article in *Eve* called 'Discovery of a Mare's Nest' and that, undoubtedly, was the inspiration for the Rupert story you can read later in this book. The dictionary definition quoted in the article says 'Mare's Nest: to find a Mare's Nest is to make what you suppose to be a great discovery, but which turns out to be all moonshine.' You can see the Mare and the King of the Birds in the 1952 endpaper and if you are lucky enough to own the annual, you will see on the back cover the Mare standing on a tree just like the one in *Eve*.

Above: The back cover of the 1952 Rupert annual
depicting the Mare's Nest

Left: Bestall's accompanying illustration to the article
'Discovery of a Mare's Nest' published in *Eve*, 1926

In 1947, three Surbiton girl guides turned up on Alfred's doorstep and asked to be
included in the Rupert stories. Thus Beryl, Pauline, Janet and Dinkie (Beryl's little
black cat) were introduced. You can see the three girl guides and also Ninky among
the figures in the 1949 cover picture. Alfred very often thought up the stories while
he was mowing the grass and then he used to draw far into the night, sitting in his
studio at the top of the house. Each frame was a little work of art. The house in
Surbiton was full of Burmese memorabilia, as Alfred's father had been a Methodist
missionary there at the turn of the twentieth century. Alfred was born in Burma in
1892 and although he did not remember his early childhood there, one can feel the
strong Eastern influence on some of his stories and his characters – for instance
Pong Ping, the Chinese conjuror and Tigerlily.

Another very strong influence, particularly on his art, was the scenery in North Wales. Alfred went to school at Rydal, Colwyn Bay, on the North Wales coast, and he visited the area almost every year (except during the First World War when he was a driver/mechanic in Flanders). For the last 30 years of his life, he owned a cottage in Snowdonia and those landscapes can be seen in some of his covers and endpapers. The cottage (called Penlan) is still being enjoyed by ourselves, our children and our four grandsons.

Nutwood is an amalgam of Surrey, North Wales and the Cotswolds in between. The Rupert stories always have a happy ending, with Rupert returning home to his long-suffering parents and the security of Nutwood. Alfred himself was a gentle, kindly man who always seemed able to see the best in people and situations. When one of our sons had a rather bad school report, he commented "I'm glad to see the boy has spirit." Rupert has spirit too.

Alfred Edmeades Bestall at work

SKETCHBOOK

These previously unpublished sketches by Alfred Bestall have rarely been seen by anyone outside the Bestall family. Egmont would like to thank John Beck, Secretary of the Followers of Rupert, for his assistance in trying to date these early illustrations.

Rupert Flying a Kite
Illustrated circa 1950.

Rupert Swinging on a Tree
A possible sketch for the 1953 annual that featured the Green Buzzer and Miranda.
The back cover sketch bears a striking resemblance to the published version.

Rupert and the Cooking Pot
A possible cover sketch for the 1950 annual that featured the Gooseberry Fool.
The character never reappeared in future annuals.

Rupert and the Girl Guides
Illustrated circa 1950. The girl guides made their debut in the 1950 annual.

RUPERT

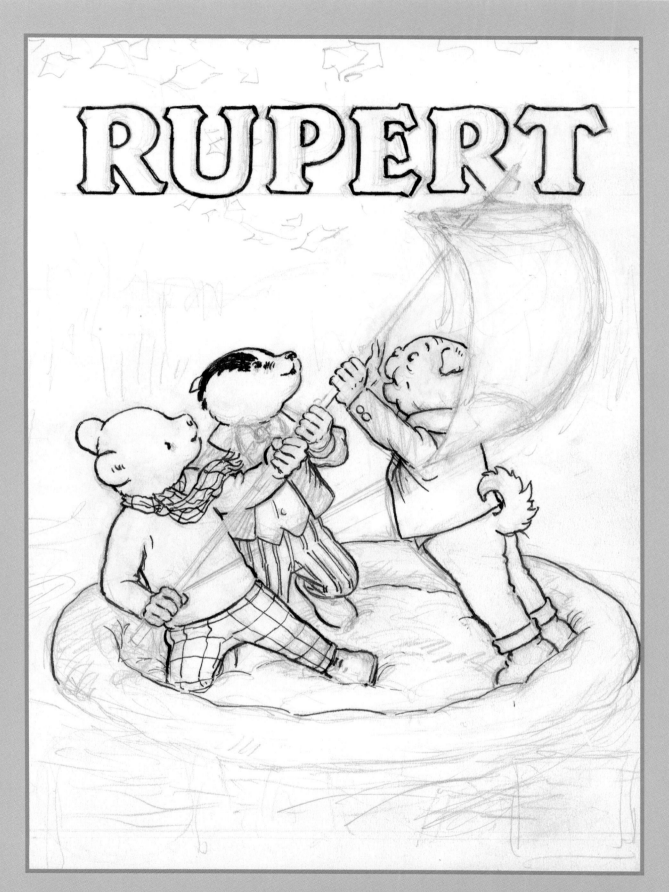

Rupert, Bill Badger and Algy Pug

RUPERT and the TINY FLUTE

How Rupert's
discovery of
the Flute stopped
the Imps doing
their work.

Spring has arrived and the meadows are ablaze with flowers. At one point Rupert notices some tall plants waving. At first he takes no notice. Then all at once he stares intently. "That's very odd," he murmurs. "There's not a breath of wind. What can be making those plants move?"

As Rupert gathers flowers one day,
He is surprised to see them sway.

He pushes through the grass to see what was making the plant wave about. He sees a hole in the ground nearby. "I suppose it was only a rabbit," he mutters. As he moves away he sees a slender stick lying at his feet which he examines closely in growing astonishment.

He finds a hole and then, nearby
A tiny stick catches his eye.

The little stick is hollow and has several neat holes in it. Wandering away, he comes across his friend Horace, the hedgehog, and shows him the whistle. Horace only gives a queer chuckle. "Never mind who it belongs to," he says. "You take my advice and leave the thing alone."

He shows the hedgehog his new prize,
"I wouldn't touch that!" Horace cries.

Rupert can get no further explanation out of Horace, and in another moment the hedgehog has disappeared. Leaning back against a post, he tries to play the thing, but he can't produce a sound. As he pauses he hears a laugh close behind him.

Though Rupert blows, he gets no sound;
A laugh behind makes him look round.

A stranger leans upon the stile,
Watching his efforts with a smile.

Turning quickly, Rupert sees a traveller leaning over the fence and smiling at him. "Oh, please, do show me how to play this little whistle," begs the little bear. The other takes it and examines it closely. "But it isn't really a whistle at all," he says. "It's a flute, and it's a little beauty."

After many attempts to play he suddenly succeeds, and a high sweet note echoes across the hill. In another instant an extraordinary thing happens, for after shaking violently, the fence flies to pieces and collapses, toppling the traveller heavily on to his back.

"Oh! Can you play it?" Rupert cries.
"I'll do my best," the man replies.

But when the stranger starts to play,
The fence begins to rock and sway.

While the traveller picks himself up stiffly, Rupert retrieves the little flute. "It's very extraordinary," gasps the little bear. "That fence looked perfectly sound." But the man is inclined to blame Rupert for his troubles and scowls at him threateningly.

Rupert again examines the fence, but can't find any explanation of the queer thing that has happened. "Anyway, the traveller showed me how to play the flute, and now I'm going to try for myself."

The man has had an awful scare,
And first of all blames Rupert Bear.

Then Rupert thinks he'll try again,
As Podgy comes along the lane.

So seating himself on a bank he holds it in the right position and puffs into the right hole. Rupert perseveres with his efforts to play the tiny flute, not noticing that his pal, Podgy, is coming to join him.

Just as Podgy arrives Rupert suddenly succeeds in blowing a shrill note. At the same moment another odd thing happens, for, without warning, Rupert shoots forward off the bank straight on to his friend, knocking him down.

But what a shock awaits him there,
His chum comes sailing through the air!

Rupert and Podgy pick themselves up carefully. "That was a poor sort of joke," complains Podgy. Rupert stares at him in amazement. "That wasn't a joke," he declares. "I was pushed off the bank." Rupert is disturbed by the strange things that have occurred, and wanders home accompanied by Podgy.

They pick themselves up, bruised and sore,
Cries Rupert, "I was pushed, I'm sure."

On the way he suddenly remembers the warning that Horace Hedgehog gave about the flute, and he tells the little pig. But Podgy only laughs. "What does Horace know about it?" he scoffs. "Why shouldn't people play it? Do let me borrow it for the night."

Then Podgy takes the flute away,
And says he'll bring it back next day.

In the middle of the night Rupert is wakened with a feeling that all is not right. Straining his ears, he hears funny little noises in the room. He determines to investigate.

The little bear wakes up that night,
Something has given him a fright.

Rupert gets up very cautiously and in his perplexity he calls out. Immediately the noises cease, and a strange little figure leaps from behind the bed and straight out of the open window. "Why, I've seen him before," murmurs Rupert. "He was one of the Imps of Spring."

No answer comes to Rupert's cry,
But like a flash an Imp leaps by.

Says Mr. Bear, "What's that I heard?"
And Rupert tells what has occurred.

Rupert's sudden call has disturbed the house. In a few moments his father appears. "What on earth's the matter?" he says anxiously. The little bear tells what has disturbed him and how the Imp has disappeared through the window.

After some more sleep he finds himself again disturbed. Opening his eyes, he sees it is broad daylight. To his amazement, the strange little sounds are once more coming from beyond the foot of the bed, slightly louder than before.

When Rupert wakes, although it's light,
He hears the sound as in the night.

This time Rupert peers over the end of the bed and gazes in astonishment at his chest of drawers. Socks, shirts and handkerchiefs keep flying out. "There must be two Imps this time, one in each drawer," he gasps. "But what can they be after, and why are they flinging my clothes about like that?"

"Oh my! What's wrong?" gasps little bear.
His clothes are flying through the air.

Rupert is now full of excitement and glides silently off the bed. With the utmost caution he creeps towards the chest of drawers and slams the smaller drawer before the other Imp knows what has happened. "Got you!" cries Rupert in triumph. "Now I will find what you're up to."

"What can the Imp be hunting for?"
He thinks, "I'll shut him in the drawer."

The door opens and Mr. Bear reappears looking very grumpy. The little bear, in great excitement, asks him to keep quiet a moment and listen. "I've got one of those Imps in here," he cries. "Let's shut the window and the door and block up the fireplace so that he can't escape."

The noise brings Mr. Bear again,
And once more Rupert must explain.

Rupert and his father close all the ways out of the room and then gently open the drawer. Instantly the Imp bounds to the top of the curtain and crouches there whimpering. "Don't be silly," says Rupert, "we won't hurt you. What are you disturbing my room for?"

The Imp is filled with great alarm,
"Come down," they coax, "we'll do no harm."

He comes at last with many sighs,
"We're looking for our flute," he cries.

Seeing that Rupert doesn't mean to hurt him, the Imp descends. "Our little flute," he sobs, "give it back to me."

"It's for calling the Imps together for any special work," exclaims the other. "It's the only flute we've got, and without it we can never hope to get through all our work."

"To us the flute means such a lot;
It is the only one we've got."

Rupert promises to get it back and return it to its rightful owners if the Imp will meet him again in two hours, and the little creature leaves him in great delight. Rupert is much too excited by the night's events to go back to bed, so he dresses and sets off to get the tiny flute back.

"All right!" cries Rupert, "never fear,
I'll get your flute and meet you here."

"You're up early," cries Willie cheerily, as they meet on a footpath. "Yes, I'm on my way to call on Podgy," says Rupert. "Well, you won't find him at home," declares Willie. "I passed him walking up that hill."

As Rupert walks to Podgy's house,
He meets his little friend, the mouse.

RUPERT AND THE TINY FLUTE

Feeling rather mystified, Rupert turns towards the hill, and at length sees Podgy sitting on some broken brickwork higher up the hill. Podgy turns with surprise. "What's brought you out so early?" he asks. "Put that thing down before there is trouble," pants Rupert. He is too out of breath to explain about the Imps.

So Rupert hurries on until
He finds his chum up on the hill.

"I'm determined to play this thing," declares the other, putting the flute into position. Suddenly he succeeds in blowing a loud, shrill note. Immediately the old brickwork shakes and collapses, and Podgy topples backwards out of sight.

As Podgy plays a note, the wall
On which he's sitting, starts to fall.

Rupert sees to his horror that poor Podgy has tumbled to the bottom. "Thank goodness I'm not killed," groans Podgy. "That flute must be a magic thing." Podgy is a good deal bruised, and declares that he is going to break the flute lest it should bring trouble to anyone else.

Then Rupert runs with great alarm
To see if Podgy's come to harm.

"Oh, please don't do that," cries Rupert. "I've promised to return it to the Imps. Do you think you could throw it to me?" Still grumbling, Podgy stands up and the tiny flute comes sailing up straight into Rupert's hands.

"Please give the flute to me again,"
Cries Rupert, "and I will explain."

RUPERT AND THE TINY FLUTE

*"I need some help, so I'll sit here,
And play until the Imps appear."*

Rupert realises that Podgy must be helped out of the old mine, and he sighs to think how far away the village is. "I wonder if those Imps could help us," he thinks, so screwing up his courage, blows a note, and the next moment an angry little Imp is standing beside him. Rupert starts to explain, but is quickly cut short. "I know all about Podgy's trouble," cries the Imp. "It's a good thing you've brought back the flute."

He sits down and plays a lovely tune. Immediately other Imps seem to spring from behind every tuft of grass and run towards the music. Rupert watches fascinated while the little player tells them how the flute has come back to them, and he tells all about Rupert's troubles. The whole crowd moves down the slope to peer into the old mine where Podgy is prisoner.

*"That isn't right," the Imp declares
And starts to play some lively airs.*

Then they scamper round the hill and begin to unfasten cobwebs from the bushes. "How can cobwebs be of any use to us?" Rupert asks. "You don't seem to realise," says the leading Imp, "that for its weight a cobweb is about the strongest thing on earth, and we are the only people who know how to make it into rope."

To help poor Podgy they agree,
And gather cobwebs from a tree.

When the little groups have each made a length of the cobweb rope the pieces are joined together. "Now," says the leader, "you shall see the strength of it for yourself."

Those clever Imps do not take long
To spin a rope that's fine, but strong.

In a few moments, after hard pulling, up comes poor old Podgy puffing and gasping over the edge of the hole. Rupert is astonished at the strength of the cobweb rope and begs to be told how to make it.

Then Podgy ties the rope on tight,
They pull – and he comes up all right.

But the little people only laugh and keep their secret to themselves. "Your little pals are a fine lot," laughs Podgy, "even though they did topple me into the mine."

They beg the little Imps to tell,
How they had made the rope so well.

As the little pair stroll homewards, Podgy asks Rupert who the Imps really are. "Why," says the little bear, "their job is to see that the spring flowers come up properly." An unexpected squeak makes them turn. One of the Imps is trying to catch them up.

As they stroll home, a sound they hear,
And turning, see an Imp appear.

The tiny creature leaps on to a gate. "I've been waiting for you to bring me the flute," he cries. "When you didn't turn up I came to look for you, and I've just heard of your adventure with the old mine." Suddenly he stops and, dropping down from the gate, darts behind a tree.

The Imp stops speaking suddenly,
And darts behind a nearby tree.

Rupert is puzzled by the Imp's unexpected action, but, peering through the bars of the gate, he sees old Willum, the farmer, approaching. "You're looking worried," says the little bear. "Yes, I be worried and no mistake," answers Willum sadly. "Something's gone wrong with the season this year. Here's the spring three parts finished and none of my crops are coming up."

Old Farmer Willum says, "I fear
The crops are very late this year."

The poor old man seems quite distressed, and the two pals are very sorry for him. "Your big field is on our way home," says Podgy. "Let's go and have a look at it." Rupert and Podgy accompany old Willum towards his four-acre field. As they reach a gap in the hedge they hear the old man give a cry of astonishment. "My crops!" gasps Willum.

Before they go, the little bear
Looks for the Imp, but he's not there.

"They be all coming up. They've
growed a foot this past hour! Either the
spring's gone mad or else I have." While
he is gazing spellbound, Rupert turns to
Podgy. "I believe I can explain this," he
whispers, and he leads his pal back to
the tree with the hole at the root.

The old man scarce believe his eyes,
"Look at my crops! They're up!" he cries.

Sure enough, as the pals reach the tree
the tiny Imp pops out and sits on a root,
laughing. "I heard old Willum's trouble,"
he cries, "so I dived in here and collected
some of my friends, and we pushed his
crops up for him." "Well," says Podgy,
"I always wanted to know what the work
of the Imps was, and now I know. I'll
take care not to annoy them again.
They're much too powerful."

The Imp says, "Now our flute is found,
Our work goes on below the ground."

RUPERT

THE DAILY EXPRESS ANNUAL

RUPERT
and
RAGGETY

A more bothersome bundle than Raggety would be hard to find, as Rupert quickly learns on meeting it after a storm. Keeping Raggety from mischief is too much for Rupert, but he thinks better of the odd creature when it helps forgetful Simple Simon.

"Make haste, if you are going out,"
Warns Daddy. "There are storms about."

The days are drawing out fast, and Mrs. Bear's thoughts are naturally turning to spring cleaning. "I'm going to be very busy indoors, Rupert," she says. "Will you do the shopping today?" "Hooray, of course I will!" Rupert smiles.

"I feel like a run across the Common. Wait till I get my scarf." Then his daddy chimes in. "The paper says that storms are beating up from the coast. You must take care," he murmurs. "Right-o, then I must be quicker than ever!" declares Rupert. And off he goes.

For Mummy's shopping Rupert goes,
He must not be too long, he knows.

Rupert makes good time across the Common. "The air's very quiet," he thinks. "I wonder if I really need to hurry like this. There's no sign of any storms as far as I can see." He gazes at the sky and all he notices is a flight of seagulls heading inland at great speed.

A flight of seagulls heads inland,
That means rough weather is at hand.

A few moments later he spies a caravan on lower ground. "That's Rollo and his Gipsy Granny," he murmurs. "Are they setting up camp? Or are they going to move away?"

"There's Rollo, busy with some task!
What can it be? I'll run and ask."

"A storm is brewing," Rupert's told,
"We must make sure our roof will hold."

In his curiosity Rupert turns aside to meet his old friends. Rollo is tightening strong cords across the caravan. "You look surprised, little bear," says the Gipsy Granny. "Well, we're taking care that the roof doesn't get blown off our home in the coming storm."

"Storm?" cries Rupert. "Have you been reading the newspaper forecasts too?" "Gipsies don't need to read about the weather. They just know," says the old lady. "You'd better run home quickly." And, feeling more anxious, Rupert hurries on his way.

"Then I must run, before it starts,"
Says Rupert, and away he darts.

"Hey, Simple Simon! What is wrong?
Why are you standing still so long?"

On the last slope of the Common he finds Simple Simon standing quite still and looking very worried. "What's the matter, Simon?" he asks. "Have you dropped something?"

"N-not exactly," sighs the boy, "but I've finished my shopping and now I can't get back into my house." "You should have brought a key with you," says Rupert. "Oh I did. I always do," declares Simon. "It's all by itself in a nice little blue purse!"

"I hid my purse, for special care,
But now, I can't remember where!"

Rupert cannot understand the boy.
"Well, if you've got the key why can't
you get into your house?" he asks.
"I didn't say I'd got the key," says
Simon. "I did have it and I hid it in
a safe place so that I shouldn't lose it.
Now I've been thinking and thinking,
and I can't remember where I put it!"

Says Simon as his gloom gets worse,
"Our cottage key is in that purse!"

"Oh dear, you *are* simple, aren't you!"
says Rupert, gazing around. Then he
pulls himself together. "I must push on,
and you'd better take shelter," he calls.
"The gipsies say that storms are coming."

"Take shelter, for the gipsies say
A dreadful storm is on its way!"

But Simon just sits down and groans,
"I'm shut out of our house," he moans.

Instead of trying to look for shelter poor Simple Simon sits down still trying to think. "My daddy will be returning soon, and if I can't remember where I hid the key we shall both be shut out," he moans. "Well, I'm afraid I can't do your remembering for you!" says Rupert. "Now I really must be off."

And this time he runs on without stopping, so that he reaches the shop quite breathless. "Whew! I've raced the storm so far!" he gasps at length. When he has recovered his breath Rupert does his shopping and tells of the gipsies' warning of storms.

"So far, the storm has not begun!"
Gasps Rupert, breathless from his run.

But now the wind is rising fast,
A cloud of dust and leaves swirls past.

Hardly has he finished when there is a rushing sound, the door swings open, leaves and dust are swirled past, and the shopman starts forward. "The gipsies were right," he declares. "You'd better stay here awhile until it's over." "No, I mustn't wait," says Rupert. "Mummy wants the things. And the paper said that more storms were coming."

And he presses on sturdily homewards. The first gusts of wind become less strong as Rupert reaches the Common. "I wonder how I'd better go," he muses.

"The storm won't break just yet, I hope!"
Pants Rupert, racing down the slope.

Then, "What's that dreadful roaring sound?"
He trembles, glancing sharply round.

"There's a footpath going round below the higher ground. It's rather longer, but it may be more sheltered." Hardly has he turned when there comes a roaring noise, and in fright he dodges behind a big tree.

Then he stops in surprise, for three tiny figures are also there. "Surely you're the Imps of Spring?" he gasps. "What are *you* doing here?" The Imps of Spring seem in a hurry to dive into a thick copse though one waits to answer Rupert.

As Rupert crouches down in fright,
Three Imps of Spring pop into sight!

"You ask what *we're* doing here," cries the Imp. "It's our job to work in the spring. But what are you doing out on a day like this?" "I'm taking this longer path to my home," says Rupert. "Well, don't do it," says the Imp, "take the shortest possible way over the Common and *hurry*! There's a storm coming such as you have never seen!"

"Run home! You heard that frightful din?
It means the storm will soon begin!"

He disappears and the little bear changes direction again. With more and more difficulty, Rupert pushes himself up the slope of the Common.

"This is the quickest route to choose!"
Puffs Rupert. "There's no time to lose!"

The roaring noise comes again louder than ever, and a hurricane of wind crashes against the hillside so that he has to bend almost to the ground to move at all. "This is awful," he puffs. "I wonder if that Imp knew that I should get such a head wind when he told me to come this way."

The gale screams louder all the time,
Against its force he cannot climb.

Near him he sees a large solitary tree resisting the gale. "That's a good shelter," he thinks. While Rupert waits the wind howls and shrieks past him, and he presses as near to the sheltering tree as he can. With his ear close to the bark, he notices creaking noises. "My, even this great tree is having to bend to such a gale!" he breathes.

Then crawling sideways in despair,
He finds a tree, and shelters there.

Suddenly the most violent roar of wind thunders over the hill, and he glances up in fright. Then he jumps and dashes to one side.

While all around the wild wind shrieks,
The great tree sways, then bends and creaks!

He is just in time for, with a loud rending noise and a snapping of roots, the heavy tree topples crazily and comes crashing down.

As Rupert makes a frantic dash,
It falls with a tremendous crash!

After the crash Rupert remains face
downward, too scared to move.

Gasps Rupert, "It can't hurt me now!
I must crawl back to it somehow."

The fury of the gale makes him wonder
if he is going to be blown away, and at
length he realises that the tree cannot
hurt him now, and that it may still give
him shelter, so, clutching at the grass for
safety, he crawls back close to the trunk.

Then past his face a live thing shoots!
It looks just like a mass of roots!

Hardly has he reached it when an odd shape seems to jump past him. "What ever's that?" he thinks. "It looks like a mass of roots, but it seems alive!" While Rupert looks on, the odd-shaped creature alights and scrabbles around as if trying to get under the fallen trunk.

Beneath the trunk it scrapes and digs,
Cries Rupert, "Is it made of twigs?"

Then it turns, and, to his astonishment, he sees that it has a crooked, crumpled face and spiky arms and legs. "How dare you!" it cries in a harsh, creaking voice. "How *dare* you pull down that old tree and break up my home? Who are you, anyway? No, don't answer. I hate you, whoever you are!"

The spiky thing turns round and glares,
"You pulled that tree down!" it declares.

And Rupert, who has never seen anything like this before, can't think what to say. The fierce wind drops very suddenly and in the calm that follows Rupert starts to ask the queer little stranger where it has come from and why it is so angry.

Then all at once the fierce wind drops,
And round the trunk that creature hops.

Instead of answering it stops its wild talk and gropes among the earth and broken roots. "My beautiful, comfy nest!" it whines. "After all these years, and I'll never be able to live there any more." "What *do* you mean?" asks Rupert. "Do you live underground? Are there any more of you?" Once again the odd spiky creature does not answer.

"My lovely nest! My comfy nook!
It's finished, done for! Just you look!"

"You broke my home up! You're to blame!
I hate you! It's a horrid shame!"

It pushes in and out of the tangle of broken roots until, with a peevish exclamation, it leaves the hole and leaps up and down in front of Rupert. "I tell you my home is done for!" Its thin, screechy voice is more angry than ever. "And, of course, you did it! There was nobody else in sight." "Oh, I *didn't!*" Rupert insists. "It was that awful *storm*, and . . ."

But the creature has turned and dashed away, looking just like a bundle of twigs. Rupert gazes after the extraordinary little stranger until it has disappeared on the lower ground. "Well, what on earth was that?" he breathes.

"Oh my," gasps Rupert, "that was grim!
I hope I've seen the last of him!"

The little bear looks round and blinks,
"My basket's blown away!" he thinks.

"It wasn't a person and it wasn't an animal and – oh dear, what am I doing? That storm has made me forget my errand." He gazes around, but his shopping basket has disappeared. "It must have been blown away," he mutters.

He hurries downhill, and at length he spies some of his parcels lying on the grass. Before long Rupert finds all his parcels, though there is no sign of the basket.

He soon finds where his parcels are,
And hopes the basket won't be far.

Then, glancing to one side, he again spies Simple Simon sheltering under a bank and clutching his hat. "Don't look so frightened," says Rupert. "The storm seems to be over and, tell me, did you see a queer raggety thing dash past here just now?" "Did you say Raggety?" says Simon gloomily.

"I thought that storm would never pass!"
Calls Simon, huddled on the grass.

"Yes, that's a good name for the thing. I saw it too. It went that way. But I was too worried about the storm that nearly blew me off my feet and my lost key to notice it much."

"A spiky thing dashed past me, yes!
It did look queer, I must confess."

"Now, where has Mummy's basket gone?"
Frowns Rupert, as he wanders on.

Simple Simon begs Rupert to stay and help him look for his missing key in its blue purse, but the little bear thinks it is more important to look for his mummy's basket that was blown away, so he asks the boy to excuse him and he presses on. Peering over a bank, his eye is caught by something further down, and hurrying forward he sees the basket.

The raggety creature, having found it, is gnawing the handle. "Hi, stop that!" Rupert calls as he runs forward to rescue the basket. "What, you again!" cries the crotchety little stranger.

"That spiky creature's found it first!"
He whispers, and expects the worst.

"Why can't you let me alone? Let go of this thing. It's mine. I found it and I want it!" "It isn't yours. It belongs to my mummy," declares Rupert as he insists on taking the basket and repacking it.

"Let go, I say! This basket's mine!
I tried it, and it tasted fine!"

At that, the queer spiky creature gets into a terrible tantrum. "Oh, how I hate you and everybody and everything," it screams.

Into a rage the creature flies,
"You horrid, spiteful thing!" it cries.

When the weird creature stops screaming it just sits and scowls. "Oh dear, I wish you'd say who you are," sighs Rupert. "I called you Raggety. What is your real name?" "Name? I've got no name! What's the good of names?" Raggety frowns. "And I've no home and nowhere to go."

Then calming down, it sits and scowls,
"I'm homeless – thanks to you!" it growls.

Rupert begins to feel almost sorry for the disagreeable little object. "Well, would you like to come and see my home and let's think about it?" he says. And, much to his surprise, Raggety grumpily agrees to go with him.

"Cheer up! I'll take you home with me,
And I shall call you Raggety."

Mrs. Bear has been worried by the great storm and is in the garden watching for Rupert's return when she starts back and stares as an extraordinary thing crawls up on the garden gate and glares at her. "Don't be frightened, Mummy," Rupert calls when he sees her expression. "It's Raggety. I don't know anything about him except that he has no home, so I thought perhaps he could come here for a bit and . . ."

"That's Raggety! I'm here as well!"
Calls Rupert. "I've so much to tell!"

But before he can finish Raggety has dropped from the gate and scurried into the cottage. Mrs. Bear is very nervous at the appearance of the creature that Rupert has brought home and she stops in the garden. However, Rupert himself hurries into the cottage.

The cottage door is open wide,
And Raggety runs straight inside!

As Rupert creeps along the hall,
He hears a sudden startled call.

At first there is nothing to be seen.
Then his daddy's voice calling out in
alarm comes from the nearest room and
he peers round the door.

He is just in time to see that Raggety,
who has climbed up the back of an
armchair, where Mr. Bear sat reading, has
seized his pipe and is throwing it away!

"My pipe!" gasps Daddy, in alarm,
He has not seen that spiky arm!

The pipe has sailed across the room and right underneath another armchair, and when Mrs. Bear comes in she finds Rupert trying to reach it.

"I'll get it, Daddy," Rupert says,
"My, Raggety has naughty ways!"

"What on earth's going on here?" she exclaims, seeing the smoke. "Yes, and how did my pipe fly over there?" gasps Mr. Bear, who has not seen the mischievous stranger. Rupert holds up the pipe.

"He's gone! Let's hope he won't return,"
Sighs Mrs. Bear, in great concern.

"It was Raggety," he exclaims. "He's just come with me and he's rather wild." "Eh, what?" says Mr. Bear. "What's Raggety? And where is he now?" All three gaze round, but in the excitement Raggety has slipped out of sight again, so they sit down to a meal and Rupert tries to explain his very curious adventure.

A sound in the next room is heard,
Cries Daddy, "Now what has occurred?"

Suddenly a slight sound makes him jump up and run into the next room, where a terrible sight meets his eyes. A flowerpot in the window has been overturned and the soil is pouring out, and beside it sits Raggety. He is holding a fine hyacinth that has been in the pot and is eating away its roots!

"That's Mummy's hyacinth you've got!
How dare you pull it from its pot!"

When Rupert darts forward to save the hyacinth the angry little creature drops to the floor and faces him afresh. "Must you *always* interfere with what I'm doing?" The creaking little voice is trembling with rage. "Those roots taste lovely and I'm hungry and, o-o-ooh, you are horrible!"

"Those roots were jolly good to eat!"
Screams Raggety. "You've spoiled my treat!"

All at once Raggety darts from sight as Mummy enters. "What ever *has* happened?" she cries. "That dreadful mess! What's the good of my spring cleaning if this sort of thing goes on?" Rupert clears up all the soil that has fallen on the floor and Mrs. Bear replants the beautiful flower though she sadly fears it will not grow again.

Then Mummy gasps, "Whatever next!"
The damage makes her feel so vexed.

"Your spiky friend has left once more,"
Says Daddy, pointing to the door.

"I'd better find out where Raggety is," says Rupert. "He doesn't seem to be able to do anything but mischief."

But this time, although he looks right through the cottage, he can see no trace of the creature. "Look, Mummy left the door ajar," says Mr. Bear. "Perhaps he's run out." So Rupert puts on his scarf and sets off to search.

So Rupert sets off on his track,
He means to bring the culprit back!

Rupert sees no sign of Raggety outside,
but just when he re-enters the garden
he hears a scratching noise as the
creature appears from somewhere and
scowls at him from the top of the gate.
"So *there* you are," cries Rupert.

He hears a growl, and turns to find
That naughty creature, just behind.

"Where have you been? And what's
that you're holding? Oh, this is too bad!
You've stolen my daddy's pipe *again*.
Drop it this minute!" Instead of obeying
Rupert, Raggety turns the other way
before dodging aside and scampering
off. Raggety leads Rupert right across
the Common, swerving and jerking
awkwardly.

"Bring back that pipe! You're in disgrace!"
Cries Rupert, swiftly giving chase.

"Oh dear," he mutters, out of puff,
"I simply can't run fast enough."

"What an aggravating thing he is," puffs the little bear. "When I want to hurry he crawls and when I want to catch him he goes like anything." After a time the odd creature puts on a spurt and disappears over a bank.

Reaching the spot, Rupert looks around. "Hello, there's poor Simple Simon again!" he murmurs. "That means he still can't remember where he hid his front-door key. Hey, Simon!" he calls. Hearing Rupert behind him, Simon turns rather wearily.

"Hello, there's Simon once again,
He's not remembered yet, it's plain."

"Have you come to help me think where I may have hidden my key?" he asks anxiously. "No, I'm chasing Raggety again," says Rupert. "What, are you *still* after that raggety thing?" says Simon. "Is he worth all this chasing?" "You don't understand!" cries Rupert. "I took him to my cottage and now he's stolen my daddy's pipe. Can't wait! Goodbye."

"I still can't find my purse, you know,"
Sighs Simple Simon, full of woe.

He hurries on and, farther away, to his relief, he spies Raggety perched on a bramble bush and staring at him. Rupert sees that Raggety is still holding the pipe. "Come on, you've had your game," he calls. "Give me that thing. It's no use to you."

Then Rupert, after further search,
Spies Raggety upon his perch.

"This pipe's a nasty, smelly thing!"
Snorts Raggety, and gives a fling.

"No, and it's no use to you either," declares the peevish creature. "Nasty, smelly thing! It was making smoke and smoke means fire and fire's the one thing I *can't* abide. Tcha! Let's lose it." With a flick the pipe is tossed away. Rupert gasps as it drops into a thicker bush.

Rupert sees his daddy's pipe drop right into the heart of the second bramble patch and he immediately tries to work his way in to rescue it. "This is tough," he mutters as the strong thorns catch him, and, though he turns as carefully as he can, he is soon unable to move either backwards or forwards.

"It's dropped into this bramble patch!
Oh dear, these thorns do cling and scratch!"

When Rupert calls out, "Help, I'm stuck!"
The creature grins, "That's just your luck!"

"Here, come and help me!" he gasps. But Raggety, who has been watching with a grin, now lets out a harsh cackle and jumps away, and Rupert continues struggling.

All at once the pressure eases. Rupert struggles out and, looking around, he sees that three of the Imps of Spring have returned to help him by pulling the branches away.

Some Imps have noticed Rupert's plight,
And now they run to put things right.

"How ever did you get stuck like that, you silly little bear?" the leading Imp demands. "It was Raggety's fault," says Rupert. "He threw my daddy's pipe in there and I was trying to fetch it out."

The little bear pours out his thanks,
Then tells about that creature's pranks.

"Well, here it is," says another Imp, crawling into the brambles and bringing it out. "But who is Raggety? Another pal of yours?"

"Well, here's the pipe! Don't look so glum!
Now, pray describe your naughty chum."

Rupert hurriedly describes Raggety. "He lost his home among the roots of that tree that the wind blew down," he says. "He looks rather like a bundle of roots himself, and . . ." "But you shouldn't play with a creature like that!" exclaims the leading Imp.

The leading Imp looks so dismayed,
And cries, "That's bad news, I'm afraid."

"He isn't safe. You never know what he may do!" "I *wasn't* playing with him," Rupert insists. "He was rather horrid, and he stole my daddy's pipe. And he jeered at me when I got stuck in the thorns." "Never mind that," the Imps sound nervous. "The point is, where is he now? We don't like him."

"We think he is some kind of Troll.
Come, join us on this grassy knoll!"

"A Troll's a special kind of gnome,
Beneath old trees it makes its home."

Rupert gathers the Imps of Spring around him. "You seem to know a lot about Raggety," he says. "Tell me, what is he? I've never seen anything like him before." "He must be some kind of Troll," says the leading Imp.

"They live under the old trees and eat the roots until the trees come down. Trolls never do any good to anybody." One of the Imps has wandered away. Suddenly he cries out.

Another Imp calls out, "Come here!
I've had a wonderful idea!"

The other Imps and Rupert hurry across the glade. "Look," says the Imp who has called them. "Here's an old tree, and it has a hollow not far from the ground. Just right for Trolls. If your Raggety would consent to live in there we could get on with our work free from his mischief-making."

"This hollow runs deep down the tree.
It's just the home for Raggety!"

"I wish I knew where he is now," says Rupert. "I'd show it to him." As they pause, wondering what to do next, a scratching noise in a bush makes them turn.

Before the others can reply,
A scratching noise is heard, close by.

Then Raggety, with one swift leap,
Dives straight into the hole so deep.

Next instant all three of the Imps of Spring have vanished. There is another rustle in the bush, and Raggety himself leaps out, moving faster than at any time since Rupert met him. Straight for the tree he goes, and dives head first into the dark space.

"The sly creature!" gasps Rupert. "He must have been watching us all the time!" Then there is a lively scrabbling noise from inside the tree, and the Imps return in time to see showers of dirt and rotten wood being tossed out from the hollow.

"He's clearing out the rotten wood!
That shows he means to stay for good!"

The rubbish flies this way and that,
And with it something blue and flat.

Some of the rubbish thrown out by Raggety nearly hits Rupert, and in one shower a little blue object flashes past him. The Imps see it too and they cluster round.

"It's plain that your Raggety is going to make his home down under that tree," says the leading Imp. "So we shan't be bothered with him any more. But what is the blue thing he tossed out?" Rupert picks it up eagerly and feels it carefully.

Gasps Rupert, "Well I never did!
It's Simon's purse – the one he hid!"

Then he rises to his feet with a happy cry. "Well, of all things," he says, "this is a real good joke!" Rupert opens the flat object and inside, as he expects, is a key. "You said that Trolls never did any good to anyone," he chuckles, "so this is probably the first good turn that Raggety ever did to anybody, and the joke is that he did it without knowing it!"

"Yes! Here's the key, inside it still!"
He tells the others, with a thrill.

And he tells them of Simple Simon and the lost purse. "This hollow tree must be where he hid it for safety. Then he forgot where he put it!" Saying goodbye to the friendly Imps he dashes away.

"Goodbye!" he calls, then full of joy,
He dashes off to find the boy.

"Now to find Simple Simon again," thinks Rupert. "I wonder if he is still in the same place and feeling miserable." He makes his way through the wood to the spot where he last saw Simon and he calls for his pal. "Hmm, he's not here," he mutters. "Will he have gone back to the shop? I'd better go and wait for him at his own cottage. He's sure to turn up there sometime."

"Has he gone home, by any chance?"
Says Rupert, with an anxious glance.

However, when he comes in sight of Simon's home he sees that the boy is already standing there and that his daddy is there, too. Shouting at the top of his voice Rupert races to his astonished friends.

"He's with his daddy, by their gate!"
And Rupert runs at such a rate.

"I've found your purse! The key's here too!"
He laughs, then tells his story through.

"You are just in time," cries Simon's daddy when he has got over the shock of surprise. "I was just going to break a window to get into my own home! But how on earth did *you* find the key when Simon couldn't?"

He opens up the cottage and when they are all sitting down to a fine tea, Rupert tells them all about Raggety and how he did them such a good turn in spite of himself.

"Oh no," smiles Rupert, "don't praise me!
Just thank that naughty Raggety!"

"Come and have a game of cricket," says Bill Badger, as he wheels his cycle up to where his pal is sitting. "Right-o, but I must finish this chapter first," says Rupert. "I'll be just five minutes. In the meantime I'll set you a competition. Your name begins with a B. Look around and see if you can find 20 other things beginning with B."

Can you find the 20 things in five minutes?
There are more than 20 in the picture.

RUPERT
AND THE MARE'S NEST

How Rupert's kindness
to birds was rewarded by
a holiday at the seaside.

RUPERT AND THE MARE'S NEST

Summer is beginning and a cool bright day has arrived, the sort of day that makes little bears want to skip about and climb trees, so Rupert, after getting his scarf and asking permission of Mrs. Bear, scampers off in search of adventure.

It is a lovely sunny day,
And Rupert hurries out to play.

He hurries in the direction of the Common and soon spies two small figures running towards a stretch of woodland. "I do believe they are Freddy and Ferdy Fox," he murmurs. "What are they up to?"

He meets no friends until, at last,
He sees the Foxes, running fast.

"Do wait for me," calls Rupert, "please!
I want to go and climb some trees."

Running down the hill and across to the wood, Rupert calls out to them and they wait for him. "It's a topping day," cries the little bear. "Let's climb some trees." "Yes, that's what we're going to do," says Freddy. "Come with us. We're going birds' nesting. Look, we've got a basket to carry home the eggs."

But Rupert steps back. "I love climbing trees," he says. "But why rob the nests? I don't think the birds would care much for that." But the Foxes only laugh at him and move away as if they don't know what he is talking about.

The Foxes say, "We're going too,
But we shall take some birds' eggs too."

RUPERT AND THE MARE'S NEST

Rupert tries hard to persuade the Foxes
to change their plans, but they run into
the woods and are soon out of sight.
When he turns away he is startled by
the shrill little bird perched on a twig.

A little bird thanks Rupert Bear,
For grumbling at that greedy pair.

"Good for you, Rupert!" it chirrups.
"I heard every word you said when you
tried to stop those two robbing nests.
Perhaps we can do you a good turn
one day."

Now Rupert thinks, "It's strange to me,
I wonder where my pals can be?"

RUPERT AND THE MARE'S NEST

So feeling rather lonely there,
He hurries home to Mr. Bear.

It flies off as quickly as it came and as Rupert can find no other friend on the Common he decides to go home.

Seeing one of his father's books on the ground he flops down and opens it. "Why are grown-up books so queer?" he thinks. Suddenly he spells out a word and jumps up in excitement.

They settle down to read and rest,
Till Rupert sees the words – "Mare's Nest".

Rupert and the Mare's Nest

"Daddy, do tell me," he cries, "what is a Mare's Nest?" To his surprise Mr. Bear, now very comfortably reading his paper in a hammock that he has fastened between two trees, smiles and doesn't answer at once. "What an awkward question," he grins, "goodness knows what you will be asking next." Rupert persists in his question and Mr. Bear sighs.

"Please tell me what it means," he cries,
"There's no such thing," his dad replies.

"A Mare's Nest, did you say?" he smiles. "That's difficult. A Mare's Nest? Well, it's the sort of thing you look for and it's not there!" "You're teasing me, Daddy," laughs Rupert. "It must be there sometimes. It's in this book of yours! But a mare isn't a bird. How can it have a nest?" Mr. Bear gets out of his hammock. "I tell you what," he says.

He smiles, then says, "Bring one to me,
And I will take you to the sea."

RUPERT AND THE MARE'S NEST

So Rupert hurries out again,
To find his friends and then explain.

"Suppose you and your pals go and search and if you can find me a Mare's Nest I'll take you away for a whole week's holiday at the seaside." Full of excitement Rupert hurries off again and this time he spies two more of his pals, Algy Pug and Willie Mouse. "I say, chaps," he calls, "have you seen a Mare's Nest. My daddy says he will take me to the seaside if I can show him one, so I must find one!"

"That's silly," says the little mouse, "how can there be such a thing?" and he strolls away. Algy, however, gets an idea and points across to some buildings. As Rupert and Algy cross the fields, Algy explains. "This is where Farmer Green lives," he says. "He may be able to help you."

"I'll help you," Algy says, "let's go
And ask them at the farm below."

*The pug explains as they draw near,
"I know that Farmer Green lives here."*

Sure enough they soon meet the Farmer and he greets them cheerily. "We're hunting for a Mare's Nest," says Rupert. "And we thought you'd be certain to tell us where to find one."

To his amazement both Farmer Green and his mare burst out laughing. "Now, young Rupert," he grins, "don't you try to catch me with your tricks." Still smiling he moves away.

*The farmer laughs at their request
To help them find a real Mare's Nest.*

When the two friends return to the Common a bird flies between them. "We've been following and listening to you," squawks the little creature, "and I'm now warning you to give up this search of yours. It's dangerous."

A bird warns Rupert with alarm,
"Give up, or you may come to harm."

As the bird flutters away Algy looks glum. "This idea of yours doesn't seem very good, Rupert," he says, "the birds don't want us to go. I do believe Willie was right and that there is no such thing as a Mare's Nest. I'm going home." Leaving the little bear he runs off and disappears.

Then Algy looks a trifle glum,
"I'm going home," he tells his chum.

Rupert stops and thinks. "If there is no such thing as a Mare's Nest why did the bird say that it was dangerous to look for it?" he mutters. "I'm not going to give it up. I know what I'll do. I'll ask the Wise Old Owl."

"Now," Rupert thinks, "I'm worried too,
I'll ask the Wise Owl what to do."

He sets off at full-speed for the forest and meets Horace the hedgehog, but before he can speak the bird appears again and squawks in his face. "Oh dear! I wish you wouldn't follow me about," says Rupert.

He meets the hedgehog, but the bird
Returns, before they speak a word.

The bird is still very excited. "We're very grateful to you for trying to stop those people birds' nesting and we don't want you to get in trouble searching for a Mare's Nest." Rupert makes up his mind. "I want to find the Wise Old Owl," he says. "Then if he tells me to go home I'll go."

The bird has hurried back again,
To warn the bear, but all in vain.

Seeing how determined he is the bird at last flies away and Horace offers to show him where the Owl's tree is. Soon the little bear is climbing through thick leaves and branches towards the secret hollow place where he hopes to find the wisest of all birds.

"I must find Owl," says Rupert, so
The hedgehog shows him where to go.

Rupert pours out his story and the owl gazes at him solemnly. "You wish to know what a Mare's Nest is," he says. "Little bear, there are things that we know but must not tell; that is one of them especially today." Rupert stares. "Why especially today," he asks in disappointment. "I can say no more," replies the wise bird. "Now you run home and forget all about it."

The owl says with a solemn stare,
"I must not tell you, little bear."

Sadly Rupert climbs down the tree. Hearing the sound of running feet he turns as the Fox brothers dash out of the thick bushes.

Poor Rupert sadly turns away,
He'll have to leave it for today.

"Hullo, have you finished birds' nesting?" he asks. "No, don't stop us," gasps Ferdy. "Right in the middle of the wood we met a fearful great bird. It chased us and we're off." They disappear, and Rupert stares. "There are no great birds here," he thinks.

The Foxes now come dashing by,
"We've seen a dreadful bird," they cry.

But as evening comes on there is a whirr of wings and a flock of birds sweeps across the darkening sky and, with a start of surprise, he sees that one of them is an enormous creature.

What can they mean? Then Rupert sees
A huge bird fly above the trees.

RUPERT AND THE MARE'S NEST

The great flock of birds disappear into the darkness, so Rupert hurries homewards and as he goes something on the ground catches his eye. "It looks like a seal or medal," he says. "Who can have dropped it? I must show this to Daddy." Picking it up he finds it very light.

"Now," Rupert cries, "what's this I've found;
A large disc lying on the ground."

Mr. Bear greets him cheerily. "Hullo, Rupert," he calls. "Have you found me a Mare's Nest?" "Not yet," laughs Rupert, "but I've brought something else, look." "What on earth is it?" says his father. "There's a picture on it of a bird with a very long beak."

Says Mr. Bear, "What can it be?
Some kind of seal, it seems to me."

He mends the broken chain with care,
Watched by an eager little bear.

While Rupert has some supper Mr. Bear mends the broken chain. "You must take this to Constable Growler in the morning," he says. "He may know where it belongs."

Long after Rupert is in bed Mrs. Bear comes into his room. "The birds are making a terrible noise when they should be asleep," she says. They peer out into the darkness without being able to see anything. "There is certainly something queer going on," thinks Rupert.

That night, the birds make such a din,
That Mrs. Bear comes running in.

Next morning Rupert carefully packs the strange seal and sets off. "Tell Constable Growler just where you found the seal," says Mrs. Bear. "I wish we could keep it," smiles Rupert, "but it looks precious, and the person who dropped it must be worrying about it."

The seal must be returned, and so
To P.C. Growler it must go.

He notices that a blackbird after fluttering round and listening to what he says, flies rapidly towards the wood, but he thinks no more of it until his way is barred by dozens of birds who fly in his face making a great noise.

But Rupert soon has quite a shock,
For birds fly round him in a flock.

"What have you got in that parcel?"
they scream. "Show it to us at once."
Although he is startled by the crowd of
birds Rupert refuses to open the parcel.
"I'm sure it's something precious," he
says, "and I'm taking it straight to
Constable Growler."

It seems just like a horrid dream,
"We think you have our seal," they scream.

Pressing round him more furiously than
ever they drive him before them right
into the wood where, on a rock and
looking very glum, sits the largest bird
Rupert has ever seen. "That is the
creature that frightened the Foxes!" he
gasps. "Oh dear, what shall I do?"

They push him till he sees once more,
The fearsome bird he met before.

After hearing what has happened the great bird looks very stern. "They tell me that you've found something precious, little bear," he says. "If it is the seal with the picture of my king it belongs to me. It is my royal mark and I must have it this minute. If you disobey me you do so at your peril!"

He's looking very cross today,
And Rupert wants to run away.

He glares fiercely but at that instant a little bird flies forward. "Don't hurt him. He is our friend," he calls. "He tried to stop the Foxes from robbing our nests. Speak to him kindly."

A bird flies and says, "Take care!
You must not harm kind Rupert Bear."

Rupert does not doubt any longer that what is in the parcel belongs to this bird, so he unfastens the paper. On seeing the royal seal the huge bird swoops down with every sign of joy. Other birds slip it over his head and he proudly returns to his rock.

When Rupert holds the seal on high,
The huge bird gives a joyful cry.

"My daddy mended the chain, but why do you wear it?" Rupert asks. "I am a carrier bird for our king and I wear this seal to show that I belong to him. Without the seal I have no power and I dare not go home."

He proudly wears the seal and chain,
Now he can do his work again.

Feeling very happy that everyone is now so friendly Rupert starts home, but he is soon stopped. "Anyone who does a good turn to our king must be rewarded," says the little bird. "By returning our precious seal you have indeed done well. What reward would you like?"

The birds explain, "You helped our king,
For you we will do anything."

Rupert thinks quickly. "What I really want to see is a Mare's Nest," he says. "The Old Owl and the others birds wouldn't help. Will the carrier show me one?" The bird pauses then tells him to climb on a nearby branch.

"Oh good!" cries Rupert Bear with glee,
"A Mare's Nest I should like to see."

To Rupert's astonishment the great bird moves underneath the branch and tells him to let himself down. "You will be quite safe on my back, little bear," he says. "What you have asked is too difficult for me. Only our king can allow anyone to see a Mare's Nest. We must go and see what he says about it."

The large bird says, "Our king will know.
Climb on my back and off we'll go."

Without delay they soar away strongly over the fields until the sea disappears. Then up they go again until they are lost in the blue and all the land disappears.

The bird sets off upon its flight,
While Rupert holds on, very tight.

They keep on flying very high,
To reach a palace in the sky.

At first Rupert is frightened at being so high in the air and on such an unsafe perch, but he finds the great bird always rights him as he slips. Higher and higher they go until, sweeping over a cloud they see a vast palace beneath them and many birds of strange shapes come to meet them.

A moment later they alight on a marble terrace and Rupert is introduced to the court chamberlain, a very important bird also wearing a seal. After hearing the story of the carrier bird's adventure the court chamberlain turns to Rupert.

The chamberlain comes out to see,
Just who these visitors can be.

He hears their tale with some surprise,
"I'll take you to our king," he cries.

"You, little bear, shall now make your bow to the king," he says. "Follow me." And leading the way into the palace he enters a brightly lit apartment, where stands a gorgeous creature clothed in ermine and wearing a crown. "That's the bird whose picture was on the seal," thinks Rupert.

But he bows low while his story is being repeated. "He shall be well rewarded," says the king. "Come, we shall take a turn on the terrace and he shall tell me his wishes."

The bird king says, "You have done well,
And now your wishes you shall tell."

RUPERT AND THE MARE'S NEST

Out on the terrace Rupert eagerly tells of his search for the Mare's Nest, and at first the king looks rather serious. "You are a strange little bear," he says, "and you are the only person I have met who believes that there is such a thing. It is a secret known only to us birds."

The king says, "I will do my best,
To grant your very strange request."

He walks about in silence for awhile, then calls his penguin attendant to him. "Go and find the court chamberlain and bid him to come to me," he orders.

Two messengers are sent to bring
The chamberlain, to see the king.

The king says, "You may help this bear,
And give him my royal seal to wear."

"I think the matter can be arranged. This little bear has met with my favour," says the king to the chamberlain. "Therefore I have decided that his strange wish shall be granted. He shall see the Mare's Nest. Make sure that he wears a royal seal for his own safety."

The chamberlain looks surprised, but he bows to the king and sets off briskly, leading Rupert to another part of the palace while the king's own attendants march with them. "I knew I was right," says the little bear. "We shan't be long now!"

The chamberlain cries, "Follow me!"
And Rupert does so, eagerly.

RUPERT AND THE MARE'S NEST

Taking Rupert into a small office the court chamberlain explains his orders. Then the penguin retires and the little bear is left facing a business-like bird wearing large spectacles, who silently hangs a seal round his neck. "I am the king's secretary," he says.

They go into an office, where
The secretary meets the bear.

"His orders must be obeyed and this sparrow will guide you to the Mare's Nest. You are in danger, but you are a brave little bear and that seal will keep you safe."

A sparrow is to lead the way,
So off they go, without delay.

RUPERT AND THE MARE'S NEST

Leaving the palace by a small door the sparrow leads Rupert down a steep slope of broken rock and tells him to scramble up. At the top, the little bear sees a pile of sticks perched on an isolated pinnacle of rock.

The way is up a rocky slope,
But Rupert follows, full of hope.

"There you are," says the sparrow in a scared voice. "Now you've seen a Mare's Nest. I'm off, you find your own way back." The bird disappears leaving Rupert all alone. "How can it be a Mare's Nest," thinks the little bear. "No horse could ever get up there!"

"There is the nest!" the sparrow cries;
Then, hurriedly, away he flies.

When Rupert tries to climb the rock,
He suddenly has quite a shock.

The quick disappearance of the sparrow puzzles Rupert. "It seemed to be frightened of something," he murmurs. "But why? It's all so quiet up here." However, he notices with anxiety that no other birds are flying anywhere near the nest.

At that moment the great pile begins to creak and tremble and, to Rupert's astonishment, a horse's head appears wearing a royal seal.

The nest begins to shake about,
And then a horse's head looks out.

Almost before Rupert can cry out the animal rises to its feet, spreads a huge pair of wings and swings into the air. "So it is the Mare's Nest, and it's a flying mare!" gasps the little bear. The graceful creature sweeps towards him.

The mare has wings and takes to flight,
She is a fine and graceful sight.

"What do you mean by disturbing my rest?" she demands fiercely. "Do you not know that none may see and live." Suddenly she spies the royal crest that Rupert is wearing. "I crave your pardon, little brother," she says. "I did not see that you, too, are in the king's favour. What do you want of me?"

She lands and speaks to Rupert Bear,
"I see the royal seal you wear."

*"I am the king's royal charger, and
I carry him about his land."*

Now that he has got over his fright Rupert eagerly pours out his story. "I was searching for a Mare's Nest because my daddy told me to," says Rupert. "But please tell me who you are and why your nest is so secret?" "You may as well know," says the flying mare.

"I am the king's charger. When he visits his realm he cannot fly because he wears his ermine robes, so I carry him. Now farewell. I must tell you no more." She soars into the sky, while Rupert carefully starts back on his long journey to the palace.

*"Oh, thank you!" Rupert cries, "and now
I must climb down these rocks, somehow."*

RUPERT AND THE MARE'S NEST

Near the bottom of the slope several birds fly towards Rupert. "Good gracious, are you still alive?" cries the first one. "I'm wearing the king's seal so that kept me safe," says the little bear. "It was a wonderful sight up there," and he starts to explain how his father started him off on his adventure.

When Rupert comes, the birds fly round,
Surprised to see him safe and sound.

Then he suddenly pauses. "Oh dear, I haven't finished my work yet!" he gasps. "However can I do the rest of it?"

The little bear stands still and sighs,
"I've thought of something else," he cries.

RUPERT AND THE MARE'S NEST

"I saw that Mare's Nest, thanks to you;
But can my daddy see it too?"

Seeing Rupert's worried expression one of the guards asks Rupert what is the matter. "My daddy says there is no such thing as a Mare's Nest," says the little bear. "And he promised to take me for a week to the seaside if I can show him one. Well now I've seen one, but how on earth am I going to show him one?"

"Quite impossible, quite, quite impossible," says the guard importantly. "Come with me. It's high time you said goodbye to the king and started for home."

"Impossible," the guards reply,
"And now you'll have to say goodbye."

So Rupert hurries to the king,
To give him thanks for everything.

On reaching the king, Rupert gives him back the royal seal and tells him how safe it has kept him during his adventure. Then he explains what is worrying him. At first the king is speechless, then, at length, he smiles.

"Well, I like people who are not afraid to ask for big things," he says. "Let's see what we can do." Calling the guard, he cries, "Go to the mountains and bid my charger come to me here. I have work for her."

The king hears Rupert's further plea,
Says, "Bring my charger here to me."

He orders fruit for Rupert Bear,
While they await the flying mare.

The king laughed and ordered fine fruits to be brought. "You will not be with us much longer, little bear," he says, "but you shall not go home hungry."

During the meal the flying mare appears and alights on the terrace and bows low to the king. "I am ready," she says. "Tell me your wishes and I will fly to do them." With growing excitement Rupert listens to the unfolding of his plans.

She soon appears and bows down low,
Then says, "Your wishes I would know."

"The carrier bird who brought you also brought good account of the birds of Nutwood," says the king. "They are doing their work so well that I have decided to give them a royal scroll to show my pleasure, but the carrier bird shall not take it for me this time.

The king explains, "This scroll will tell
The Nutwood birds they pleased me well."

"Here it is sealed and finished and you, little bear, shall take it for me, and my charger will fly you and tell you the rest of the plans." "How perfectly topping!" cries Rupert, jumping with excitement. "When shall we be off? Can we start now?"

Now Rupert is to ride the mare,
And give the scroll when he is there.

The flying mare kneels so that Rupert can take his seat on her back. The next moment they are soaring high in the air, but to Rupert's surprise they spend time soaring round in circles.

The mare continues with the flight,
And will not land while it is light.

"Aren't we going to land?" he asks. "Not till night falls," replies the other. "I may not visit your land by daylight. That is not allowed." But when darkness falls she sets a straight course and glides down and down until she lands on top of a pine tree.

When darkness falls, she lands with ease
Upon the highest of the trees.

RUPERT AND THE MARE'S NEST

"You are near Nutwood Common," says the mare. "This tree is easy to climb down. The messenger of the birds will meet you and you can give him this royal scroll, then go straight to your home." "But how about showing my daddy a Mare's Nest?" asks Rupert.

Poor Rupert wears a worried frown,
He wishes he were safely down.

"You will be fetched when we are ready for you," replies the mare. The pale moon gives a little light as Rupert feels his way downwards. Suddenly he notices a dark shape floating silently round and round him.

As he gets nearer to the ground,
He sees a dark shape flying round.

The dark shape settles on the tree,
"It's Wise Owl!" Rupert shouts with glee.

Before Rupert reaches the ground the dark shape settles on a branch beside him. "Why it's the Wise Old Owl!" gasps the little bear. "Of course you are the bird that flies by night; you must be the messenger I am expecting. Look, here is the royal scroll that your king sent for all the birds of Nutwood."

"That is indeed an honour," says the owl proudly. "I saw you arrive on the king's charger. I must go to her now for orders." As Rupert reaches the edge of the wood a large shape looms up before him.

He is the messenger all right,
And takes the scroll with great delight.

Now P.C. Growler comes along,
And asks young Rupert what is wrong.

"Constable Growler," he cries happily. "Oh how glad I am to see you. It's terribly lonely in there." "And I'm glad to see you, young Rupert," says the constable. "Half the village has been searching for you for many hours."

Rupert prattles away as they make their way back to Nutwood, but the policeman cannot make head nor tail of his adventures. "Mare's Nests and such are not in my line," he says gruffly. Soon Rupert is running to meet Mr. and Mrs. Bear in his cottage.

He takes him home, as it is late,
And there his parents sadly wait.

How glad they are to see him well,
And hear the tale he has to tell.

Rupert is so excited at his adventure that he starts telling his story as soon as he gets into the cottage and though Mrs. Bear gets his supper he still goes on. "You promised to take me to the seaside if I showed you a Mare's Nest, didn't you, Daddy?" he cries.

"Well, I've seen one, I'll show you one too, later, when we are fetched tonight." Mrs. Bear stares. "No more outings tonight," she says. "It's long past your bedtime, so off you go. The whole thing sounds like a fairy tale to me."

Says Mrs. Bear, "It's time for bed,
Be off with you, you sleepy head."

RUPERT AND THE MARE'S NEST

Rupert undresses very slowly and while he has his bath and prepares for bed he thinks about his adventure. Just as he is getting between the sheets a sharp noise makes him start.

A sound now reaches Rupert's ear,
Perhaps the messenger is here?

The next moment he is out of the room and searching for his father. "Daddy, Daddy," he calls, "I told you that we should be fetched tonight, and somebody's tapping at my window." "Good gracious, why aren't you asleep hours ago?" grumbles Mr. Bear. "I suppose I'd better come."

He hurries down the stairs again,
To find his father and explain.

"It is the owl!" he cries with glee,
"And now the Mare's Nest you shall see."

Mr. Bear pulls back Rupert's curtains and opens the window. Next moment a silent shape glides towards the light and settles on the sill. "Look, look!" cries Rupert. "It's the Wise Old Owl.

"He's the messenger and he must have come for us to go and see the Mare's Nest. Do let's go straight away!" The owl doesn't say a word but gazes steadily at Mr. Bear. Then, with a loud hoot, it glides back into the night.

Says Mr. Bear; "It's late, you know;
But still, to please you, I will go."

Poor Mrs. Bear is worried too,
When told what they propose to do.

"Well this beats me," says Mr. Bear. "You said we should be called and I suppose we'd better go, though what your mother will say I can't imagine." Mrs. Bear is horrified at Rupert going out again so late, but when she hears the full story she sighs and then wraps warm shawls around Rupert, putting his dressing gown over them.

Soon the little bear is perched on his father's shoulder, and the owl, who has waited for them, leads the way in the moonlight through the forest.

They find the Wise Old Owl outside,
He's waiting there to be their guide.

RUPERT AND THE MARE'S NEST

In the middle of the forest Rupert stops and points. "There you are, Daddy," he cries. "That tall tree! D'you see it? There's a great pile of sticks and branches right at the top of it and now I've shown you a Mare's Nest!" "How do I know it's a Mare's Nest?" murmurs Mr. Bear, staring hard. As he speaks a great creature rises from it and, standing black against the sky, it spreads its wings.

He leads them straight back to the tree,
The Mare's Nest is quite plain to see.

Then it soars away and is lost to sight. The next moment the owl is beside them, ready to lead them both home again.

The mare flies off, as they stand there;
"How wonderful!" gasps Mr. Bear.

Next morning Mr. Bear is sure,
He dreamed it all the night before.

After the excitement of the night Mrs. Bear brings Rupert his breakfast in bed and his father sits by him. "That Mare's Nest was the most wonderful thing," says Mr. Bear. "So wonderful that I'm not sure that we weren't dreaming or whether we really saw it."

When he is dressed Rupert insists on going to the forest. Before long they stop and gaze around. "I can't make out where the owl led us," says Mr. Bear. "Everything looks quite different this morning."

So, after breakfast, back they go,
But now, the place they do not know.

They search around, but all in vain,
They cannot find the nest again.

Rupert and his father search but can find no trace of the track that they followed in the middle of the night. "I'm beginning to think we were dreaming," says Mr. Bear. "We'd better go home again."

Just as they are leaving the wood, a loud chirrup interrupts them. "Just a minute, Rupert," pipes the little creature. "You did us a good turn once when you tried to stop those foxes. Now perhaps I can do one for you."

A tiny bird to Rupert flies,
"I'll help you if you like," he cries.

The little bird has heard all about Rupert's disappointment and offers to guide them to where they want to go. In great excitement Rupert takes his father's hand and drags him back to follow their leader.

In great excitement, off they run,
"What luck!" laughs Rupert. "This is fun."

At length Mr. Bear stops and points. "That's it!" he cries. "That's the tree we saw last night, but, look, there's no sign of the Mare's Nest. We must have been dreaming after all!" Rupert stares in bewilderment, but the little bird whispers, "Go nearer to the tree."

But when they find the tree – oh dear,
The nest has disappeared, I fear.

Now when they start to look around,
The nest is scattered on the ground.

Following the advice of the little bird, Rupert and his father go nearer the tree and all round the foot of it they see a ring of sticks and branches of all shapes and sizes.

Mr. Bear looks closely at them. "This is a pine tree," he says, "but these are not pine branches. They must have been brought here." Here the bird joins in. "You're quite right," it pipes. "No one has ever seen a Mare's Nest. The mare always kicks them to pieces before daybreak."

The bird explains, "That's all you'll find.
She never leaves her nest behind."

*Now Mr. Bear says, "I agree,
You've earned your visit to the sea."*

Rupert and his father start homewards. "Remember," chirrups the little bird, "if ever you see a tree surrounded by branches that don't belong, it's a sure sign that a Mare's Nest has been there the night before."

"Well," says Mr. Bear in astonishment, "you have done what I thought nobody could do, Rupert. You have shown me a Mare's Nest, and now I'll carry out my promise and we'll have a jolly week at the seaside." And they go straight to the station to find out the times of the trains to Rocky Bay.

*They go to ask, that very day,
About the trains to Rocky Bay.*

"I say, you chaps," says Rupert, "I've just found a short cut up to the windmill."
"Don't tell us," cries Bill, "let Algy and me try to find it for ourselves!"
"Right-o, be off with you," says Rupert. "Only remember this: you mustn't get
in the river and there must be no breaking through any hedges. The gates are
all open, but Farmer Wurzel says that nobody must set foot in any field that
contains a red board." Algy scampers down and over a bridge, but Bill decides
not to cross the water. Which of them finds the short cut?

RUPERT
and the
LOST CUCKOO

It is one of the busiest birds in
Nutwood Village, and how
Rupert misses its cheery voice!
After a long search he discovers
why it has vanished from its
usual home.

RUPERT AND THE LOST CUCKOO

One morning in August, Rupert is walking on the Common when he hears an unusual noise. "This place is always quiet," he thinks. "I wonder what is happening." Climbing a low bank he spies a group of birds fluttering and chattering excitedly.

Says Rupert, "What a noisy crowd!
I can't think why they chirp so loud!"

At the sight of him they fly away and, as he hurries forward, Rupert sees them join a larger flight high in the sky. "Different kinds of birds don't generally fly together like that," he murmurs. "Something is happening. What can the excitement be?"

Though Rupert wishes they would stay,
The birds are scared, and fly away.

"One bird has turned – I wonder why,"
Says Rupert, gazing at the sky.

As Rupert watches the sky, one of the birds separates itself from the flight and glides downwards. Something odd about its shape makes him gaze at it intently as it settles on a distant fence.

Creeping round the bushes inquisitively on tiptoe, he manages to get quite near without disturbing it. "Why, surely it's a wooden bird!" he gasps. In his surprise he moves a branch, startling the queer creature which flaps creakily away in the direction of the village.

A closer view makes Rupert blink,
Says he, "It's made of wood, I think!"

He tries to keep the bird in sight,
But soon it vanishes in flight.

Hurrying forward to keep the stranger in sight, Rupert meets his pals Rastus and Lily Duckling, but they haven't noticed it and don't seem very interested, so he scampers home.

"Guess what I've seen, Mummy," he cries, "a live wooden bird, a real one. It flew this way and it was carrying a spray of leaves in its beak. What d'you think it can be?"

Puffs Rupert, breathless from his run,
"I've seen a bird – a wooden one!"

"Yes," Rupert nods, "I'm sure it's true,
Its wings were creaking as it flew!"

"You must be dreaming," smiles Mrs. Bear, who is busy preparing dinner. "Are you sure you haven't been sleeping out on the Common?" Rupert gets very excited as he continues his story. "I really did see a wooden bird," he insists. "It came this way and its wings creaked as it flew." Mrs. Bear looks thoughtful. "Did you say it creaked?" she murmurs.

"I heard a curious creaking noise in this very cottage not long ago. I wonder . . ." Leading the way past the cuckoo clock in the hall she looks in the other rooms. The windows are open, but there is no sign of any stranger in the house, and all is quiet.

Says Mrs. Bear, "That's rather queer,
For I've heard creaking noises here."

"The blackberries are nice and sweet,
So will you pick us some to eat?"

A thorough search of the cottage reveals nothing out of order and at length Mrs. Bear sends Rupert out again. "There should be plenty of blackberries about now," she says. "Will you pick me a nice basketful?"

So away he races back to the Common. "Hullo, there's another flight of birds," he exclaims. "And one of them is a very odd shape. It's not a bit like that wooden bird. I wonder what it can be. And where are they going? They seem to be heading for the lake." There is no shortage of blackberries, and Rupert is soon busy.

"Those birds are heading for the lake,"
Says Rupert. "What a noise they make!"

Before he has filled the basket there is a gentle snuffling noise and Horace the hedgehog appears. "Hullo, you're just the person to explain what is happening," cries the little bear. "I've seen such strange birds. They were . . ."

Asks Rupert, "Did you see them pass?"
As Horace shuffles through the grass.

"Talking of birds, there is something queer going on," Horace interrupts. "Can you hear what I can hear?" Rupert listens, and from behind him comes the call of the cuckoo, small but clear.

Then Horace hears a funny sound,
So Rupert stops and looks around.

"In August cuckoos shouldn't call,
They ought not to be here at all!"

Rupert cannot understand what Horace means. "But a cuckoo isn't queer," he says. "There are lots of them. Now these other birds I've been telling you about, they're queer. One was made of wood, and now . . ." But Horace interrupts again. "There aren't lots of cuckoos any more. Don't you know your poetry? It's August now and they've all gone. The one we heard was late."

Grumpily he disappears and Rupert, meeting Lily Duckling, asks if she has seen the wooden bird again.

Says Lily, "We've not seen or heard
A creature like that wooden bird."

RUPERT AND THE LOST CUCKOO

Back to his cottage Rupert goes,
It's time to have a meal, he knows.

Neither Lily nor Rastus has seen any more of the wooden bird so Rupert, realising that he is hungry, hurries home, where he finds Mrs. Bear in the kitchen.

"Will dinner be ready soon, Mummy?" he asks. "All in good time," she smiles. "I'll bring it in sharp at one o'clock. I'm waiting for the clock to strike!" "But it's past one o'clock," cries Rupert. "I looked as I came through the hall." "Surely it can't be," says Mrs. Bear. "I've listened carefully and it hasn't struck yet."

Smiles Mummy, "Dinner isn't late,
The clock's not struck – you'll have to wait."

RUPERT AND THE LOST CUCKOO

Rupert is so certain of himself that Mrs. Bear, feeling very mystified, follows him into the hall. "You're quite right!" she says as she gazes at the cuckoo clock. "It's well past one o'clock, but I'm quite sure it didn't strike one. There must be something wrong with the works."

And then they hurry to the hall
To see the clock upon the wall.

But Rupert gets a sudden idea and fetching a chair he opens the little door at the top. "No wonder it wouldn't strike," he calls anxiously. "Do you see what has happened? Our cuckoo has gone!" Rupert and his mummy are bewildered.

But Rupert, standing on a chair,
Can see the cuckoo isn't there.

"Our cuckoo might be lost, you know.
I heard one call not long ago."

"A cuckoo clock isn't much use without its little bird," says Mrs. Bear. "Oh dear," moans Rupert. "I heard a cuckoo when I was on the Common just now. It had a little voice, too. D'you think it could have been our cuckoo? If so I think I know which way it went. May I go and search?"

After dinner he starts and at once he spies a group of his pals, the Rabbit twins, Bill Badger and Willie Mouse, all standing and talking earnestly.

"My pals look serious today,
And seem to have a lot to say."

"There's something puzzling all of you."
Says Rupert. "So please tell me too."

Rupert runs up to his friends. "I say, listen," he calls. "All sorts of queer things are happening! This morning I saw a wooden bird, then I saw another larger bird with a huge tail, and now, guess what! – the cuckoo out of my cuckoo clock has vanished!"

Bill gives him an odd look. "Now I'll show you a queer thing," he says. "D'you notice anything missing from the Squire's house over there?" Rupert stares. "Why, yes," he gasps. "The weathercock has gone too!"

"What's happened to the weathercock?"
Bill asks. "It gives us quite a shock."

All the little pals are excited at the disappearance of the Squire's weathercock and they scamper off to fetch Constable Growler. "Ay, 'tis gone. It must have fell down like," he says gravely. "Come, we'll tell the Squire and then you shall help me to look for it."

Old Growler looks up with a frown,
And thinks the thing has fallen down.

But Rupert stays behind. "That bird with the big tail that I saw," he mutters. "It was just the shape of a weathercock. Oh dear, what does it mean? First the wooden bird, then my cuckoo – and now this! Something strange is happening."

Soon Rupert's left to puzzle out
Just what the mystery's about.

RUPERT AND THE LOST CUCKOO

None of Rupert's friends seems to be able to explain anything, so he determines to try by himself to find out why such mysterious things have been happening. He calls out to some birds that he sees returning from the lake, but they do not stop to answer him.

Although the birds hear Rupert's call,
They do not answer him at all.

At length he finds one resting on a branch. "Do please tell me," he begs. "What are the birds doing today? I saw a wooden one this morning and now the cuckoo from my cuckoo clock and the Squire's weathercock have gone!" At first the bird does not answer.

"Ah, there's a bird perched on a tree!
Perhaps he will explain to me."

Then it looks rather annoyed. "You're not very clever," it squawks. "Surely you knew that that wooden bird was the dove out of Mr. Noah's Ark!" "Why, of course it must have been!" cries Rupert. "But what was . . ."

"That's Noah's dove – do use your eyes!"
The angry little bird replies.

"Don't ask any more silly questions!" screams the other. "That's all you need to know, isn't it?" And it flies away out of sight, leaving the little bear puzzled at the bird's annoyance and feeling even more mystified.

The little bear is at a loss
To know what's made the bird so cross.

Then Rupert gazes from the hill
To where the lake lies calm and still.

Rupert waits and ponders what the bird has said. "It sounds as if the wooden bird is the key to the mystery and if I could find it I could also find my cuckoo," he says. "That means I must find Mr. Noah. If he is in the district he must have water to float his Ark in, and the only water quiet enough is the Nutwood Lake."

He hurries up the hill until he can see the lake far below and soon he is thrusting through a thick wood on his way down. Rupert breathes with relief after he has struggled through the wood. As he pauses to get his bearings he gives a sudden start, for there, right beside him, is the wooden dove itself, standing on a branch and watching him intently.

So through the woodland, thick and dark,
He makes his way to Noah's Ark.

"Why, you're the very person I'm looking for," cries the little bear. "Please, do you know where my cuckoo is?" For a moment the dove, still holding a leaf in its beak, eyes him silently.

The dove, a twig held in its beak,
Frowns at the bear, but will not speak.

Then, without a single word, it flies rapidly away towards the lake. "Oh dear, I'm not getting very much help," sighs Rupert.

Then suddenly with wings outspread,
It flies towards the lake ahead.

Pressing onwards to the lake, Rupert finds his way barred by two large toy animals, an elephant and a giraffe, who are quickly joined by a wooden tiger. They all regard him with silent disapproval. "Are you all from the Ark?" asks Rupert.

"Do you belong to Noah too?
If so, I'd like to speak to you."

"Please, do you know if my little cuckoo came this way?" The animals look very grave. "Have you had an invitation?" asks the giraffe. Rupert is taken aback. "Invitation to what?" he says. "I don't understand. I only want my cuckoo!"

"Please, did my cuckoo come this way?"
Asks Rupert, but they will not say.

While Rupert has been speaking, several more animals have appeared and now, without answering him, they move a little distance away and stand in a solemn circle. "I wish I could hear what they are saying," murmurs Rupert. "They don't seem a bit pleased to see me."

The small giraffe speaks for the rest
And says, "Are you another guest?"

He sits down to wait and at length most of the others hurry away to the lake, leaving one who approaches Rupert. "We have decided to ask our Captain about you," it says, "so you'd better follow me. Come along."

The animals walk on again,
But one moves closer to explain.

"I'll find my cuckoo soon, I hope,"
Thinks Rupert, running down the slope.

Still feeling very bewildered Rupert follows his small leader down the last slopes of the hill. At the edge of the lake he is confronted by a little old man who looks at him gravely.

"Oh, please, are you Mr. Noah?" he says breathlessly. "Yes, I am," says the little man. "And you're Rupert, aren't you? My animals told me about you. Well, your cuckoo is quite safe, so now you can go home again." "But why did it go away?" cries Rupert. "Our clock's no good without it."

He meets a man who's white and old,
"Yes, I am Noah," he is told.

As soon as he has spoken Mr. Noah begins to walk away, but Rupert is not satisfied. "If you know where my cuckoo is won't you let me see it?" he pleads. "Has it gone for ever? Surely you don't want it for the Ark, do you?"

Says Rupert, "But our clock's no good
Without a cuckoo made of wood."

Mr. Noah turns and looks at him more kindly. "Dear me, how anxious you are," he says. "I invited your cuckoo to come here for the day, but I didn't invite you. That's why my animals want to stop you. Come, I'll tell you all about it."

"I cannot see my cuckoo – why?"
Asks Rupert with an anxious sigh.

*"Tired birds," says Noah, "come to stay
When they have earned a holiday."*

While Rupert listens Mr. Noah explains the mystery. "Every year I arrange a special picnic," he says. "And I only invite those who need it most.

"When my messenger went to Nutwood he decided that your cuckoo and the Squire's weathercock were the hardest-worked creatures in the village, so we asked them here for a day's outing and a trip on the Ark. See, there it is, just returning."

*"Trips on my Ark give them much joy,
It's coming closer now. Ahoy!"*

Up flies the dove at Noah's sign.
He says, "Go to that Ark of mine!"

"So there's no need to worry at all!" cries Rupert. "What a relief! And how very kind of you, Mr. Noah." Rupert asks Mr. Noah rather timidly if he can wait and take his cuckoo home with him. "Well," says the old man, "that is generally against my rules, but since you have taken so much trouble I may allow it just this once."

Raising his arm he calls loudly and in a few minutes his messenger, the wooden dove, flies to him. "Go to the Ark," he commands. "Tell our guests from Nutwood that the picnic is over and bid seven of our little birds to lead them here."

"I hope our guests enjoyed their fun,
But tell them that the picnic's done."

When the dove has departed on its mission Mr. Noah takes Rupert behind some bushes. "My little birds don't like strangers," he says. "If they see you too soon they may become shy and fly somewhere else."

"Now you must hide, for birds are shy,
And if they're scared, away they'll fly."

So Rupert waits out of sight and before long there is a whirring and creaking of wooden wings as the little dove appears with seven other little birds from the Ark. In their midst is a large shining bird with a huge tail.

The cuckoo's missing from the group,
As swiftly overhead they swoop.

RUPERT AND THE LOST CUCKOO

The weathercock cries, "Goodness me,
There's Rupert standing by the tree!"

"That must be the Squire's weathercock!" gasps Rupert. On spying Rupert the weathercock swerves and settles on a tree. "Why, bless my tailfeathers!" it cries in its loud brassy voice. "If it isn't you, Rupert, from Nutwood. I've never seen you so close before. You're bigger than I thought."

"So are you, much bigger than I thought," says Rupert. "But, please, I'm waiting for my cuckoo. Where is it?" "It certainly started from the Ark with us," says the other. So Rupert waits, but the cuckoo does not arrive.

"My wooden cuckoo isn't here,"
Sighs Rupert, "and he's lost, I fear."

Without delay he runs along
And tells the old man what is wrong.

After a while Rupert becomes anxious and he goes to Mr. Noah. "Please, I think something has gone wrong," he says. "You promised that your little guests from Nutwood should come to me.

"When the party of birds arrived the weathercock was among them, but there is no sign of my cuckoo and I'm worried because my clock is no good without it." Mr. Noah looks serious. "What, no cuckoo!" he cries. "I must put that right." And, waving towards the Ark, he shouts some loud orders.

Says Noah with a kindly smile,
"You'll have your cuckoo in a while."

"Though every bird's flown by at last,
My cuckoo hasn't yet come past."

Obeying Mr. Noah's command, all the remaining birds on the Ark fly ashore over Rupert's head and settle on a tree facing the old gentleman, but there is still no cuckoo. Mr. Noah tells them what has happened and for a while there is silence.

Then the messenger dove comes forward. "The cuckoo and the weathercock followed us," it declares, "but we didn't keep an eye on them because they knew the way. The tiny cuckoo must have slipped away unseen."

The dove exclaims, "Well, this could mean
Your cuckoo slipped away unseen."

The animals have searched around
But still the cuckoo isn't found!

Mr. Noah commands every bird at once to search for the missing cuckoo. Then he turns to Rupert. "They cannot search very far," he says. "In fact, except for my messenger dove, they must not go out of sight of the Ark or they might not find their way home."

One by one the birds return without having seen anything of the little truant, and at length Rupert decides he can wait no longer and turns sadly away. "What awful bad luck!" he sighs. "Just when I thought I'd got it back."

To Nutwood Rupert makes a start,
He's feeling very sad at heart.

RUPERT AND THE LOST CUCKOO

Soon Rupert stops and gives a shout,
"Hey, Horace, are you still about?"

As Rupert wanders gloomily towards Nutwood he passes the place where he picked blackberries and he calls out to see if Horace the hedgehog is still there. In a few minutes Horace shuffles into sight and listens to the sad story.

"I don't see what you're complaining about," he says grumpily. "Of course, your cuckoo has gone. Don't you remember? All cuckoos go away in the autumn!" "B-but, surely not clock-cuckoos," gasps Rupert. "Ours has never gone before!"

When Rupert's call makes Horace come,
The hedgehog says, "Don't look so glum."

Horace the hedgehog, still grumbling, moves forward. "A cuckoo's a cuckoo even if it does come out of a clock," he says, "and I expect yours has gone with the others. That's the direction they took, towards the sun, and I believe they go to a place called Africa." He turns and disappears into the bushes.

"Yes," Horace grunts, "I told you so,
He's flown to Africa, you know."

"Oh dear, this is worse than ever!" cries Rupert as he hurries back towards the lake and meets some of the animals. "I must find Mr. Noah again now that we know where we may have to look."

"I think," says Rupert, "I should tell
Old Noah where he's gone, as well."

The little bear hears Noah say
That Africa is far away.

Rupert finds Mr. Noah just as the last birds return from their unsuccessful search. "Oh please," he puffs, "Horace says that my cuckoo has probably gone to a place called Africa. D'you know where that is? And can you send your messenger dove to bring him back?"

Mr. Noah looks anxious. "That is a far country and my dove is too busy," he murmurs. Then a little bird chirps, "Cuckoos come back in the spring. Yours is sure to come with them."

"Cheer up, the warmer days will bring
Your cuckoo back again next spring."

*Just then, above them in the sky,
The weathercock goes flying by.*

Rupert is a little comforted, but not very much. All at once he spies a shining object in the sky. It is the weathercock on its way back to Nutwood. "Hi, you're just the person I want," he calls.

"You don't belong to Mr. Noah, you're free to do as you like. Please, will you fetch my cuckoo back from Africa?" "But I'm not free," says the weathercock importantly. "How do you think the Nutwood people will know which way the wind is blowing if I don't tell them? I must get back to my work. Goodbye."

*"I cannot go, so don't ask me,
I have my job to do, you see."*

Poor Rupert seems to be no nearer to finding his lost cuckoo. "Mummy will be very unhappy if we have to wait until next spring before our clock can strike again," he says. Mr. Noah too is very sorry and sends his birds up for a final search.

The little birds look everywhere,
But Rupert's cuckoo isn't there.

"Horace may have been wrong when he thought your cuckoo had gone to Africa," he suggests. But the birds, as before, have no success and at length the little bear gives it up and trudges sadly homewards.

"The cuckoo can't be found, I know,
Although they've hunted high and low."

Mrs. Bear sees Rupert coming slowly home. "Well, and what have you found out?" she asks. "Not very much I'm afraid," says Rupert. "I discovered that our cuckoo went to a picnic with Mr. Noah, but nobody has seen it since and Horace thinks it may have gone right away until next spring!"

Says Mrs. Bear, "He's lost, I fear,
But don't upset yourself, my dear."

"Well, well, if it has it can't be helped," sighs Mrs. Bear. "So don't worry too much. It must be nearly four o'clock. Let's have tea." Suddenly Rupert gives a start. "Listen, did you hear what I heard?" he gasps.

Gasps Rupert, "There is no mistake,
That's just the sound that cuckoos make!"

*"My cuckoo's back again – hooray!
He didn't really go away!"*

The next moment Rupert is capering about in glee. "Why, what ever has come over you all of a sudden?" asks Mrs. Bear mystified. "Didn't you hear?" cries Rupert. "Our cuckoo must have come back!"

Rushing into the cottage he looks at the clock. "Yes, there you are, four o'clock has just struck and it was our cuckoo's voice doing it. Quick, I must make certain." And dragging up a chair he gets level with the clock and opens the little door.

*Says Rupert, "Mummy, see the time!
I knew I heard the cuckoo chime!"*

When Rupert peeps behind the door
He finds his cuckoo, home once more.

Sure enough, as soon as the tiny door is opened the cuckoo pops its head out. "Why, where have you been?" cries Rupert. "I traced you to Mr. Noah's picnic. Then you vanished and Horace thought you had gone to Africa." "Cuckoos from clocks don't go to Africa," declares the other.

"We're much too busy! No, when I saw you at the picnic I thought you'd be angry with me, so I slipped away. And nobody noticed. And here I am!" Then it pops back, the door shuts, and Rupert is soon having his tea.

At last the family, all three
Sit down and have a lovely tea.

After tea Rupert finds the bird who first set him on the trail. "Will you tell Mr. Noah that my cuckoo came straight home?" he asks. "What a lot of fuss," squawks the bird. "All right. I'll go."

"That cuckoo gave us such a fright,
But now he's home, so that's all right!"

In the village Rupert finds his pals gazing at the Squire's house. "Do look up there," cries Bill Badger. "Nobody has been up to that turret and yet the weathercock is back in its place!" "My cuckoo's back, too," laughs Rupert. And he tells them all the story.

"The weathercock is on its spire,"
Says Rupert. "That will please the Squire."

RUPERT

WITH
EXCITING
MAGIC
PAINTING
PAGES

THE **DAILY EXPRESS** ANNUAL

RUPERT'S RAINY ADVENTURE

Telling of the floods that came and how Rupert and Sailor Sam saved baby Trunk.

Poor Rupert wishes he could play,
But here's another rainy day.

Rupert stands and gazes out into the cheerless scene. "Oh dear, I'm so tired of being kept in," he sighs. His mother's voice interrupts him. "Here, Rupert," she calls, "I've got a job for you to do."

Rupert finds his mother holding some black, shiny clothes. To his amusement she makes him put them on. "The wet weather has kept you in so long that I have bought you these," she says. "There are Wellingtons and an oilskin coat and a sou'wester; no rain can get through those. Now, I want you to run out and see how Mrs. Trunk is."

He's very glad when Mrs. Bear
Gives him an oilskin suit to wear.

He sets off feeling very gay,
And by the river makes his way.

Rupert splashes out happily into the wet
and finds that his fine new clothes really
do keep all the rain out. He follows the
path on the bank until a boathouse
comes in sight. "Hullo," he cries. "The
door's open and there's the prow of a
boat sticking out."

To his surprise his old pal Sailor Sam is
hard at work inside. "You're not going
out in all this rain, are you?" asks the little
bear. "Of course I am," laughs the other.
"Sailors don't mind a bit of bad weather.
Come in and talk to me while I put on
the last touches."

The boathouse door is open wide,
And Sailor Sam he finds inside.

*"Come in," he says, "and see my boat.
It's almost ready now to float."*

Inside the boathouse Rupert sits and chatters to his friend while the boat is completed. "Now," cries Sailor Sam, "we can take the mast down and get the little craft afloat." Rupert remembers his errand. "I'm afraid I can't go with you," he says regretfully. "I'm on my way to see Mrs. Trunk. Can you tell me where she lives?"

Sailor Sam directs Rupert to Mrs. Trunk's house. "I shouldn't care to live there myself," he says. "It's too near that old weir just up the river, and if anything happened the house would soon be in a bad way."

*"Well," Rupert says, "I cannot stay,
To Mrs. Trunk I'm on my way."*

When he draws near, the little bear
Sees Mrs. Trunk is standing there.

Rupert is hurried into the house out of the rain. "My mother was wondering how you liked your new house," he says, "and she sent me to call on you."

Mrs. Trunk, who has been preparing to bath her baby, pauses and smiles at him. To Rupert's surprise, Mrs. Trunk puts the baby down and starts to put on her outdoor clothes. "I've got to do some shopping, and until you came I had no one whom I could leave with my baby, Pompey."

Then Rupert says, "I've come to you,
In case there's something I can do."

Rupert offers to do her shopping for her, as the rain is so heavy, but she prefers to go to the village herself. Back in the house Rupert gazes uncertainly at little Pompey.

So Mrs. Trunk goes to the shops,
While Rupert with the baby stops.

He is standing silently and wondering how he can keep the baby amused when he becomes aware of a sound that he cannot understand. "I've never heard anything quite like that before," he murmurs.

"What is that rushing sound I hear?
I think it's coming from the weir."

As Rupert crosses the room the strange sound grows louder and nearer, and before he can reach the open door there is a tremendous splash; a great wall of water crashes up against the wall of the house, and comes pouring into the room. For a moment Rupert stands paralysed.

Then with a terrifying roar,
The water bursts in through the door.

When he gets his wits back Rupert's first thought is for Pompey, the baby elephant. Pompey is rather heavy, but with much effort Rupert manages to get him into his arms and then gazes round for a safe place to put him. The bath seems to be his only hope, so he dumps the baby inside just before his strength gives out.

He lifts the baby off the ground,
Into the bath, quite safe and sound.

Thinks Rupert, "I'll get out of here,
Or else we shall be trapped, I fear."

He notices the level of the water creeping higher. "If it gets beyond the door we shall get trapped against the ceiling," he cries. "We must get out." Giving the bath a push towards the doorway he scrambles in beside Pompey.

The moment Rupert and Pompey are outside the house they are caught by the flood and swirled away. At length they get into quieter waters. Pompey smiles and enjoys it all, but Rupert puts up the umbrella and wonders however they are going to get out of their troubles.

The bath is rocked from side to side,
And Pompey quite enjoys his ride.

Then suddenly a voice they hear,
It's Mrs. Trunk calling quite near.

Suddenly a cry makes him turn, and to his joy he sees Mrs. Trunk standing at the edge of the flood and waving to them. The bath makes an unwieldy boat, but Rupert hits on the idea of using the umbrella as an oar and he manages to zigzag it gradually towards her.

Rowing with the umbrella first on this side and then on that, Rupert succeeds in getting quite close to Mrs. Trunk when another current catches the bath and swirls it off. In a few minutes he is farther from the shore than ever. Glancing over his shoulder he sees that they are drifting straight for a tree.

To reach the land he tries in vain,
The current sweeps them off again.

Rupert watches anxiously as the bath heads for the tree. A boat-hook suddenly dangles in front of his nose and a cheery voice cries from above him: "Catch hold of it, Rupert, and hang on." Grabbing the boat-hook, Rupert is astonished to see his old friend Sailor Sam.

Now Rupert is relieved to see,
A boat-hook dangling from a tree.

Clinging to the boat-hook, Rupert wonders what to do next. Under Sailor Sam's orders he takes the boat-hook and lets it into the water and uses it as a punt-pole. Then, with Sailor Sam's help, he begins the difficult job of hoisting Pompey, the baby elephant, up to safety in the tree.

And Sailor Sam calls from on high,
"I'll help you up. It's nice and dry."

"Did you try out that boat of yours?" asks Rupert. The sailor grins ruefully. "This *is* the boat," he says. "She was sailing along nicely when that flood smashed the boat against this tree. I managed to save these planks and the sail and lots of cord and rope."

"Where is your boat now?" Rupert cries.
"It smashed against this tree," he sighs.

For a long time Rupert sits in the shelter telling Sailor Sam the strange story of his journey with baby Pompey in the floating bath. "It's a good thing we have the bath," says the sailor. Rupert peeps out, and to his horror the bath is floating gently away down the flood.

"Oh look!" shouts Rupert in dismay,
"The bath is floating right away."

Rupert and Sailor Sam sit gazing
dolefully out on to the flood scene
and wondering how they can get away.
At length the rain ceases, and the little
bear climbs higher up the tree. On the
edge of the flood he sees Mrs. Trunk,
who waves again when she catches
sight of him.

At last the rain stops and they see,
That Mrs. Trunk waits anxiously.

Feeling very disconsolate, Rupert climbs
higher into the branches, and a large
crow flies to him, settling on a twig. "Do
you think the water's going down at all?"
asks Rupert. "Not yet," replies the crow
cheerfully. "There's lots more to come.
But I tell you what – you write a letter
and I'll fly with it to your home. Then
perhaps they'll come and rescue you."

A friendly crow then comes in sight,
And says he'll help them in their plight.

Rupert quickly scrambles back down the branches and tells Sailor Sam of the crow's suggestion. The man turns and collects the twine and rope which he has saved from the wrecked boat.

When Sailor Sam hears of the bird,
He sets to work without a word.

Sailor Sam unrolls all the thin twine and then ties it to the end of the thicker rope. Rupert grasps it quickly. Climbing again to the upper branches, he explains the idea to the crow.

He joins some twine on to a rope,
"We'll get ashore with this, I hope."

The bird immediately flies off with the end of the light twine. Mrs. Trunk has been watching the activity in Rupert's tree with anxiety. She is very puzzled.

So Rupert climbs the tree once more,
And sends the crow off to the shore.

Then she hears Rupert's voice crying instructions. Suddenly she realises what she has to do. Seizing the twine she eases it over the branch and pulls until the thicker rope is dragged across the space.

Quite near to Mrs. Trunk he lands,
And soon their scheme she understands.

Following Sailor Sam's instructions, the crow returns to Mrs. Trunk and then flies back with the end of the thin twine in its beak. Rupert watches while the sailor skilfully fashions a strong bag from a piece of the sailcloth, puts baby Pompey into it, fastens the twine to the front of it and then hangs the lot on the rope.

Then Sailor Sam thinks of a plan
To save the baby if they can.

When all is ready they shout across the water for Mrs. Trunk to pull on the twine. Gently the contraption begins to slowly move across the space, and the baby elephant chuckles with glee.

As Mrs. Trunk pulls on the twine,
Her baby slides along the line.

Now Rupert is the next to land,
He climbs the rope, hand over hand.

Now it is Rupert's turn. The crow has flown away, so they can't get the bag back to their tree, and the little bear gazes awestruck at the swirling water below, but, screwing up his courage, he swings out on to the rope. Hanging upside down, he grasps firmly and crawls hand over hand to safety.

Arriving at the end of the rope Rupert drops thankfully on to the grass and then turns to watch Sailor Sam crawl across to join him. Soon they are both standing beside Mrs. Trunk and baby Pompey. Rupert and Sailor Sam race to the weir, keeping their eyes on the missing bath. "That's a bit of luck," shouts the sailor. "The bar is preventing the bath from being swept away."

Then as they walk along the path,
They come across the baby's bath.

Stepping carefully, he crosses the swollen river and then hauls the bath back. Pulling the bath ashore, Sailor Sam puts it in a shed, and the little party reach Nutwood without further trouble.

Old Sailor Sam climbs on the weir,
While Rupert watches him with fear.

Mrs. Trunk is full of praise for Rupert. "What would have happened to my baby Pompey when the flood came if Rupert hadn't taken care of him?" she cried.

They're glad to be safe home again,
From their adventure in the rain.

RUPERT

The **DAILY EXPRESS** Annual

RUPERT and NINKY

Telling how a little girl's
mischief puzzled Santa Claus
and how Rupert solved
the mystery.

"What pretty curtains," Rupert cries,
"They really are a nice surprise."

"I'm getting tired of these shabby old flowered curtains," says Mrs. Bear one day. "Daddy has brought me this bright new cloth so we'll have a change." She gets very busy and soon Rupert is helping her to take the old ones down and put up fresh ones.

"This is grand," says the little bear. "It makes the room look twice as bright." Then he is quiet and thoughtful for a moment. "My pal, Bill Badger, is not very well," he says. "May I go across to his cottage and ask if he's better?"

His mother says, "I like them too,
And these will make a suit for you!"

Outside it is very cold and Rupert has to hurry to reach Bill's cottage. Mrs. Badger opens the door to him and looks very worried. "You can't see Bill," she says. "He's not at all well today; come back again in a day or two." "Oh, I am sorry," cries Rupert.

When Rupert goes to call on Bill,
He finds his little chum is ill.

"I'll run home and think what present I can bring for him." When he has nearly reached his cottage the driving snow whips into his face with such force that he doesn't notice another figure on ahead of him.

Quite suddenly it starts to snow,
And Rupert has to bend down low.

*He very nearly fails to see
A little girl beneath a tree.*

In a few moments Rupert nearly collides with the other figure; it is Tigerlily, the conjurer's daughter. Then Rupert has an idea. "Why not come to see my mummy until the snow stops?" he smiles.

Rupert brings Tigerlily into his home and Mrs. Bear welcomes her cheerfully. "You can give me some ideas," she says. "I'm wondering what to make with this flowered cloth." "Why not make some curtains?" says Tigerlily. "But they are curtains," cries Rupert. "Mummy has just taken them down."

*It's Tigerlily standing there,
So home they go to Mrs. Bear.*

Rupert wanders round the room wondering what to get for Bill, and Tigerlily goes from one to the other trying to help but getting no ideas. At length Rupert glances at the mantelpiece and he smiles. "I say, Mummy," he cries. "That little old china donkey – can I take that as a present for Bill?"

A china donkey Rupert spies,
"I'm sure that would please Bill," he cries.

"No, Rupert," says Mrs. Bear. "You can't have the china donkey, but I'll make a lovely cloth donkey for Bill out of this old curtain. If I only had some proper stuffing for it."

But Mrs. Bear says, "That will break;
A lovely cloth one I will make."

"Me got lovely stuffing for donkey if Rupert come and get it," smiles the little Chinese girl. So Rupert eagerly puts on his coat again and the two friends set off.

They have no stuffing there, and so
To Tigerlily's house they go.

"Come with me," says Tigerlily. She leads the way down to an underground storeroom and from a box she lifts an armful of soft cotton wool. Rupert touches it. Then he draws back sharply. "Oo! It does feel funny," he chuckles. "It sends a queer tingle through my fingers and all the way up my arm!"

She finds a box that's packed quite full
With lots of fluffy cotton wool.

So Rupert puts some in a sack,
Then thanks his chum and hurries back.

Mrs. Bear is delighted with the stuffing and grasps it eagerly. In two days the cloth donkey is finished and Rupert gazes at it in delight.

"Don't you think he has a nice kind face?" smiles Mrs. Bear. "He's a fine donkey," laughs Mr. Bear, "but he doesn't look very brainy, does he? In fact I think he looks a bit of a nincompoop." "Oo, what a lovely word," cries Rupert. "I don't know what it means, but I shall call him Ninky for short. I'll ask Bill to call him Ninky, too."

They all agree, when it is done,
The donkey is a splendid one.

RUPERT AND NINKY

Rupert writes a card to go with his
present to Bill and then he takes paper
and string to tie up the cloth donkey.
He tugs the paper round it, but when
he tries to tie it, the string keeps slipping
off. "Well, whatever's the matter with
the thing?" he cries. "You'd almost
think it was alive."

As Rupert sits upon the ground,
He feels the parcel twisting round.

The parcel is so awkward that Rupert
gives up, and taking Ninky out of the
paper he stands him on his feet. Almost
at once the cloth donkey gives a twitch,
then another, then he leaps in the air.

At last he gives up in despair,
And Ninky springs into the air.

But now the donkey stands quite still,
So Rupert takes him off to Bill.

Rupert grabs Ninky and sets him on his feet again, but this time the donkey does not move. He only stands calmly gazing into the fire. "It's a complete mystery to me," declares Mrs. Bear. "Anyone would think he was alive."

"Well, I'll see what Bill thinks about it," says Rupert, "but I shall not wrap him up, I'll hold him tight under my arm." Putting on his coat he sets off, and soon he is sitting on Bill's bed listening to his pal's delighted thanks for bringing him such a lovely present.

Bill Badger claps his hands with glee,
"How kind of you to think of me."

Hardly has Bill spoken, when Ninky gives a twitch and before they can recover their wits the little donkey has jerked himself right out through the open window. Rupert runs to the window, climbs on a chair and leans out.

Then Ninky, to their great dismay,
Leaps through the window and away.

Ninky has landed on his feet, taken three or four more jumps and then fallen over on his side in the snow. "This is just stupid," says Rupert. "If he were alive he wouldn't topple over and lie there like that." He scrambles over the windowsill and runs to Ninky.

"How strange," gasps Rupert in surprise,
"He's lying on the ground," he cries.

Rupert makes up his mind to ask Tigerlily and her father for an explanation. Before he has gone far he sees a small parcel lying near the path in the snow. Picking up the parcel, Rupert sees Mrs. Sheep going back from the village with a heavy basket.

"Hi, Mrs. Sheep!" cries Rupert Bear,
"Is that your parcel lying there?"

He hurries to return it to her and she is very grateful. "I'm getting too old for carrying such heavy packages," says the old lady. "I wish I could carry them for you," says Rupert, "but I'm terribly worried about that cloth donkey."

She says, "Oh thank you, that is kind.
I should have left that one behind."

Mrs. Sheep is much mystified at what Rupert says. "I wish I could see him jump," smiles the old lady. They both look at him, and at that moment Ninky gives a convulsive leap, bangs hard into Mrs. Sheep's shopping basket and strews the contents all over the snow.

Now Ninky jumps up from the ground
And knocks the parcels all around.

"I'm terribly sorry," says Rupert. "I do hope nothing is broken. You see what I meant about that cloth donkey?" The old lady is much shaken. "It's a dangerous toy," she quavers. "Your mother should take it to pieces again."

Poor Mrs. Sheep says with alarm,
"That toy of yours will do some harm."

Rupert says goodbye and stoops to lift Ninky. Then he gets a shock, for the cloth donkey is not there and is nowhere to be seen. Rupert reaches a gap in the hedge and scrambles through, gazing round eagerly for any sign of his little donkey.

The little bear has such a fright,
For Ninky, now, has vanished quite.

"He can't have jumped right across that great field," he murmurs. Two lines of footmarks are in sight and the little bear looks at them in excitement. "One set is coming to the hedge and the other set is going away," he says, "but neither of them belongs to Ninky."

At first his footprints are quite clear,
But suddenly they disappear.

A whirring noise comes from the air,
And Rupert sees a 'plane up there.

Rupert trots swiftly over the snow, but before he has gone far another surprise awaits him, for there is a curious whirring noise and a little 'plane rises from behind a slope and shoots over his head.

On the far side of the field he spies his friend, Edward Trunk, and he goes over to him. "Did you see whose 'plane that was?" he asks. "Yes, it belonged to a queer little chap like a sort of Boy Scout," says Edward. "He was carrying some sort of animal under his arm."

Then Edward Trunk comes to explain
That Ninky went off in the 'plane.

Poor Rupert cries and rubs his eyes,
"I'll never get him back," he sighs.

Rupert wanders home and sadly tells his mother the whole disappointing story. "I did so want to find out why he jumped," he whispers. "Well, I shouldn't cry about it," says Mrs. Bear.

The next morning, while Rupert is having breakfast, he is listening carefully for a certain sound. Sure enough, soon afterwards that same whirring noise which he heard before reaches his ears and he dashes to the window just in time to see the 'plane nearing the earth. "It's come back," he shouts, and rushes out.

Next day, to Rupert's great delight,
The little 'plane comes into sight.

Rupert sees a little figure like a Boy Scout alighting just as Edward described. "Oh, please," he cries, "who are you? Where are you from? Have you got my donkey, Ninky?" The little figure stares.

When Rupert hurriedly runs out,
He sees a rather strange Boy Scout.

"I did find a donkey yesterday," he says, "but you weren't there." "Yes, but he's mine," says Rupert anxiously. "Where is he? Is he still in your little 'plane over there?" "I'm a Toy Scout," says the little fellow. "I go scouting for new kinds of toys, and your cloth donkey took my fancy."

He says, "I came here yesterday
And took your funny toy away."

*"I work for Santa Claus, you see.
I wish you would come back with me."*

The little Scout sees that Rupert is mystified, so he goes on explaining, "I belong to Santa Claus," he says, "and he sends me scouting for new toys which children may like at Christmas." And he invites Rupert to enter the 'plane.

Rupert is delighted to be taken where Ninky is, so he clambers in behind the Scout and with the familiar whirr they rise into the sky. "This 'plane's very quiet. Is it a toy one?" asks Rupert. "Yes, it's the most powerful one that Santa Claus has got," says the little fellow.

*"Oh yes, I'd love to!" Rupert cries,
And soon they're flying through the skies.*

Skimming gracefully over the battlements of the castle, the small 'plane alights on a lofty courtyard and at once a Toy Soldier on guard comes marching up.

A sentry says when they get there,
"You cannot enter, Rupert Bear!"

The Toy Scout goes straight to the office of Santa Claus and explains why he has brought Rupert. "Hullo, Rupert," says the old gentleman genially. "Does this queer creature belong to you? What's it made of? How does it work?" "I can't tell you much," says Rupert. "He doesn't seem to work to any rules."

But it will be all right they know,
So straight to Santa Claus they go.

He says, "I cannot make it out.
What makes your donkey jump about?"

Rupert tells Santa Claus all he knows about the cloth donkey. At that moment Ninky startles them all by shooting into the air and dropping back on the desk with a thud. "So he does work," gasps Santa Claus.

Ninky doesn't move again, and at length Santa Claus gets up. "This animal worries me," he says. "I can't give donkeys like that to children next Christmas unless they can control his jumps. He might jump into their bath or into their porridge at breakfast."

Says Santa Claus, "Please go along,
To ask the storeman what is wrong."

RUPERT AND NINKY

Santa Claus goes back into his office, and Rupert takes Ninky while the Toy Scout leads the way through passages and corridors and then turns abruptly into quite a small office with a few toys arranged neatly on shelves.

The rooms and corridors are vast,
And Rupert's rushed along too fast.

An aged doll with a quill behind his ear comes to meet them. "This is the storekeeper. Put your donkey down, Rupert, and see if he can explain why he jumps," says the Scout. The little bear obeys and the old storekeeper bends down and looks closely.

They reach the store and there explain,
But Ninky does not jump again.

Suddenly, without any warning, Ninky leaps straight up into their faces, catching them so much by surprise that the storekeeper and the Toy Scout topple over. Before they can recover, the donkey makes another jump and disappears into the dark passage outside.

Quite suddenly, to their surprise,
He leaps so high, he nearly flies.

Rupert is the first to pull himself together. He dashes out into the passage after the truant. His eyes take a moment or two to get used to the poor light, and he is just in time to see Ninky tumble down the first steps of a spiral staircase.

Now Rupert is dismayed to find
That he is getting left behind.

Poor Ninky finds he cannot stop,
And plunges from the castle top.

Ninky continues blundering his way down the winding staircase, and at the bottom he bounces out on to a little terrace. One more awkward jump and he has landed on the parapet, where he sways for a moment before toppling right over.

Hardly knowing what to do, Rupert turns and finds that the Toy Scout has followed him down the winding stairway. "Let's go after him," says the Scout. "He has so far to fall that we will catch him before he lands." And they run for the 'plane.

The Scout hears Rupert Bear explain,
Then says, "We'll catch him in the 'plane."

So the little bear clambers in, the 'plane whirrs and rises smoothly over the battlements; then the Scout puts it into a nosedive at tremendous speed. In a few moments they see Ninky falling just in front.

They dive so quickly – what a thrill!
And there is Ninky, falling still.

"We are near him, but can we possibly catch him?" he asks anxiously. The Toy Scout puts on a little spurt and then loops sharply under Ninky so that the cloth donkey falls neatly into Rupert's arms. "That was perfect," cries the little bear. "You are clever. And now, please may we land at Nutwood?"

Just as they're almost on the ground,
They catch the donkey, safe and sound.

The Toy Scout does as Rupert has asked and lands gently near the spot where Edward Trunk had first seen him. "And now what are you going to do?" queries the Scout.

"I'll say goodbye now," Rupert sighs.
"Oh must you go?" the Scout replies.

"When you first took Ninky away I was going to see Tigerlily," says Rupert, "to ask whether she could explain why Ninky started jumping as soon as he was made. Now that I've got him again I'll go on with that idea." "Well, do let Santa Claus know the result," sighs the Scout.

The Scout flies off, then Rupert goes
To see what Tigerlily knows.

Entering the grounds, Rupert spies the tall figure of the conjurer and he runs to show him the cloth donkey. "Please can you tell me what is wrong with Ninky?" he begs. "He seems to have some magic in him."

The conjurer is waiting there,
And says he'll help the little bear.

The conjurer looks solemn. "Magic, you say?" he murmurs. "Come, we will go in, and my cat shall tell us." They enter a small room. "Place donkey on table," says the man. Rupert obeys. The cat at once begins to fidget, gazing at Ninky but refusing to go near him.

"You're right," he says, "there's magic here,
My cat is frightened to go near."

When Tigerlily comes, she cries,
"Your Ninky is a great surprise."

All at once a new voice is heard and Tigerlily's smiling face appears. "Hullo, Rupert," she says. "Me play trick. Hee-hee!" The conjurer starts and looks very stern. "Now, naughty girl," he says, "tell what you know."

Tigerlily looks very timid. "I give Rupert's mummy lots of lovely soft cotton wool from your private room so that she can stuff donkey," she whispers. "Unhappy girl," shouts the conjurer, but Rupert suddenly interrupts. "Please don't scold," he pleads. "She tried to be kind."

Her father shouts, "So it was you!
That was a naughty thing to do."

When Rupert speaks the conjurer gives a sigh and stops scolding. Reaching a slender jar from a shelf he tosses up a handful of sparkling dust so that it falls on and around the little donkey. The conjurer replaces the slender jar on his shelf.

He sprinkles stardust, shining bright,
Then says, "That ought to put things right."

"There, little bear," he says. "Your donkey now full of good magic. He no jump too high and he only jump when you tell him." "Oh, do let me try," cries Rupert. "Jump! Ninky." At once the little donkey bounces about six inches off the table.

Now Ninky is as good as gold,
He only jumps when he is told.

Now that Ninky is in proper order Rupert thanks the conjurer and declares that it is time to return home. Tigerlily gets her cloak to see Rupert home, her father ties a Chinese lantern to a long pole, and the procession moves steadily across the snowy Common.

"Oh thank you," Rupert says with joy;
Then hurries home to show his toy.

Rupert at last gets home and his mother is delighted to see him. The little bear shows her Ninky's new tricks and tells her the wonderful story of his journey to the clouds, finishing with a description of the conjurer's stardust.

He has a thrilling tale to tell
And writes to Santa Claus as well.

The next morning Rupert starts off with the letter to Santa Claus when he hears the whirr of the toy 'plane. The Scout lands and hears Rupert explain what has happened. "Well, it's a pity there will never be another donkey like Ninky," he says, "but it's been great fun."

Next day the Scout is back again,
So takes the letter in his 'plane.

When the Toy Scout has soared into the clouds with the letter for Santa Claus, Rupert runs to Mrs. Badger's cottage and for the second time makes Bill a present of the cloth donkey.

When Bill receives his toy once more,
He's more delighted than before.

The RUPERT BOOK

THE DAILY EXPRESS ANNUAL

RUPERT'S CHRISTMAS TREE

A story that shows how Rupert learned that it was wrong to be too inquisitive.

Christmas is drawing near. Rupert is making out a list of the presents he means to give to his friends. All at once he gets an idea. "I say, Mummy," he cries, "I think I'll have all my pals here for a party! Then we could hang their presents on a Christmas tree and they'd get them all at the same time."

Says Rupert, "Christmas now is near,
Please may I have a party here?"

Mrs. Bear smiles. "Where's your Christmas tree coming from?" she asks. Rupert is so keen on his idea that Mrs. Bear, going to the lumber room, discovers a little old wooden tub and a good deal of coloured paper. "Now for the Christmas tree," says Rupert. "I know nothing about that," says Mrs. Bear. "You'd better ask your father."

When Mrs. Bear says that he may,
He sets to work without delay.

Now Rupert and his Dad agree,
That they must have a Christmas tree.

So, seizing his scarf, he runs to find
Mr. Bear and tells him all about his
preparations. "You're quite right," says
Mr. Bear. "Let's plan out where you had
better go and begin your search."

Mr. Bear goes to the shed and brings out
an especially small spade. "If you do
find a Christmas tree, don't break it or
chop it down," he says. "Dig it up
carefully, then it may live and we can
put it in the ground again later."

Says Mr. Bear, "This spade is light,
To dig your tree it is just right."

RUPERT'S CHRISTMAS TREE

To Nutwood Common runs the bear,
But finds no Christmas tree up there.

"It's a real puzzle!" murmurs Rupert. "Where do all the Christmas trees come from?" He spies the figure of a man with two dogs in a field below him. "That must be Farmer Green," he says. "I'll ask him if he has any on his land." Farmer Green welcomes Rupert and is amused at his search.

"It's a long time since I was young enough to look for a Christmas tree," he smiles. Then he leads the little bear to a gate and points up a hill. "If you can find a tree small enough for you, you can dig it up and take it home."

Says Farmer Green, "That is my wood.
I'll let you look there, if you're good."

Thinking his search is nearly over,
Rupert plunges into the pine wood.
He threads his way in and out and gazes
sharply all round for a Christmas tree,
but has no luck. "This is extraordinary,"
he murmurs. "I could never dig up one
of these and, anyway, they'd be much
too big. There doesn't seem to be a
young spruce tree in the whole wood!"

Though Rupert searches all around,
There's not one spruce tree to be found.

Rupert, feeling very disappointed,
wanders out into the open and up to a
rocky little piece of high ground. "Oh,
dear," he sighs, "I never imagined that
Christmas trees were so scarce." After
watching the smoke for a while Rupert's
curiosity is aroused.

He feels so glum until he sees,
A wisp of smoke among the trees.

The little bear soon finds the place,
But of the culprit there's no trace.

"I've seen nobody else except Farmer Green since I came out," he murmurs, "and I've heard nobody. I wonder if that's a gipsy fire." While he gazes at the ashes a sound reaches his ears. "I do believe that is someone shouting for help!" he cries.

While Rupert listens, the sound comes again, and he turns to run in the direction of it. He reaches rocky ground which ends in a cliff. Peering over the edge, he sees a tangle of briars and brambles, out of which a pair of legs are waving.

Then Rupert hears a muffled cry,
And finds the cause of it near by.

Rupert runs along the clifftop until he finds a way down and then he works round to the bramble patch. Standing on a rock, he grabs some long briars and, despite the prickles, he pulls them away, while the prisoner, who turns out to be a very odd-looking little man, struggles to free himself.

The poor man's in a bramble patch,
Oh dear! – how they do tear and scratch.

"I was running away from you because I run away from everybody," he says mysteriously. "You're the first person who has seen me for years and years." Rupert stares at him and then he tells all about his search for a Christmas tree.

The little man asks Rupert Bear,
To tell him what he's doing there.

*And then he says, "A place I know,
But you must not see where we go."*

When Rupert has told his story the odd little man laughs gently. "You have done me a good turn, little bear," he says. "And now, if you will promise not to ask too many questions, I'll get you a Christmas tree." Taking out a large handkerchief, he blindfolds Rupert.

Rupert finds himself led over a very rough path and soon the little man takes off the handkerchief that has blindfolded him. To his amazement Rupert sees that he is standing at the entrance to a rocky tunnel and ahead of him is a whole forest of young spruce trees.

*They soon arrive and Rupert sees,
Long rows and rows of Christmas trees.*

Now Rupert is surprised to hear,
A squeaky little voice quite near.

Rupert trots gaily forward and almost at once finds a tree of the size he needs. "That will exactly fit the tub," he chuckles. He is just about to dig it out when a voice makes him stop. "Go away, you mustn't do that," it cries. While Rupert gazes round, the odd little man reappears.

"Who was that calling?" asks the little bear. "Never you mind," says the man. "I told you this was a secret wood and you mustn't ask questions. If that's the tree you want you've only to say so. Come, you must go back now, and I'll tell you just what you must do."

The little man will not explain,
But says they must go back again.

He tells the bear just one thing more;
To leave the tub outside his door.

The queer little man again blindfolds Rupert and leads him back through the tunnel. Before he takes off the handkerchief he tells the little bear just what he must do. "When you get home," he says, "you must fill that tub with some good soil and leave it outside your cottage until it has been dark for an hour or two. That's all."

Racing home, Rupert finds that his father has brought the decorated tub outside. "That's right," cries the little bear. "When it is full we must leave it here until two hours after dark." Mr. Bear looks up in surprise.

"The tree is coming!" Rupert cries.
"What do you mean?" his dad replies.

RUPERT'S CHRISTMAS TREE

So Rupert tells where he has been,
And of the strange things he has seen.

When Rupert is having his supper of bread and milk he tells his father and mother all about his search. "I don't know where the secret forest is," he says, "because I was blindfolded when I went, but the little keeper of the wood told me to fill the tub and leave it outside and wait for the Christmas tree."

Two hours after dark, Rupert begs his father to take him to look at the tub. "It's all nonsense," grumbles Mr. Bear, but he gets his torch and out they go. As they round the corner there, in the tub, is the Christmas tree!

"Oh look!" they gasp, "the tree is here.
Who could have brought it?" This is queer.

They take it in to Mrs. Bear,
Who has the decorations there.

With much puffing and grunting Mr. Bear lifts the Christmas tree and carries it into the living room where Mrs. Bear has just collected all the ornaments to decorate it. "What a lovely little tree," she says, "how did it get there?" Rupert sighs happily. "Nobody knows," he replies.

"May I go down first thing in the morning and hang the decorations on the branches?" he asks. "Then we'll know how many more there will be room for." Mrs. Bear smiles. "Very well," she says. So, at last, Rupert gets into bed.

By now it's very late, and so
To bed the little bear must go.

RUPERT'S CHRISTMAS TREE

Rupert wakes early and calls his parents, and they go down to put the ornaments on the Christmas tree. In the doorway they stop and stare in astonishment, for the tree is sparkling and brilliant. "But how did it happen?" shouts Rupert. "Someone has finished our work for us!"

Next day they are amazed to see,
The decorations on the tree.

Rupert and his parents walk round and round the Christmas tree, but cannot solve the mystery. So he bustles around, and when the party arrives all his pals gaze with delight at the beautiful things hanging on the branches.

The tree is such a lovely sight,
That Rupert's chums gaze with delight.

They really do have lots of fun,
And all too soon the party's done.

As Rupert is pulling a cracker with Tigerlily, the conjurer's daughter, he has a sudden idea. "You and your father do magic and marvellous things," he says eagerly. "Did you have anything to do with the tree?" But Tigerlily smilingly shakes her head. "Me no do it, and my daddy no do it. Me know nothing," she says.

The party ends and, tired and happy, Rupert's little friends go home. Just as the last one has gone and he has shut the front door, he hears a small high-pitched laugh behind him. There is nothing in sight except the Christmas tree.

A funny little laugh they hear,
But Rupert finds no one is near.

RUPERT'S CHRISTMAS TREE

Rupert cannot sleep after so much excitement. He lies and puzzles over the queer things that have happened, the strange voices, the arrival of the Christmas tree, the way the decorations got on to it. Just then a tiny noise reaches his ears and he sits up, listening intently.

As Rupert lies awake that night,
Again that voice gives him a fright.

By and by it comes again. "Something's happening downstairs," he whispers. Rupert creeps out of bed and puts on his dressing gown. Opening the window he leans out into the cold air. Sure enough there is a little scratchy noise in the dark shadows.

He thinks the voice came from the ground,
And so he looks without a sound.

Feeling his way downstairs in the dark Rupert is surprised to find the living room door open, but a bigger shock awaits him when he switches on the light. There on the table is the little tub. The decorations that had been on the Christmas tree are strewn around it, but of the Christmas tree itself there is no sign.

Now Rupert stares in great surprise,
"The tree has gone again!" he cries.

It has vanished! Switching on the passage light, he gives another gasp. "The front door's open too," he whispers. "It must have been opened from the inside." The trail of soil leads through it and straight down the garden path.

Out in the dark runs Rupert Bear,
He must find out who has been there.

RUPERT'S CHRISTMAS TREE

Rupert soon finds that following a trail in the middle of the night is not easy once he is away from the glow of light in his own cottage. The next moment something appears up the slope, black against the night sky. "That's the tree," he cries, "and it's moving. But who's carrying it?"

It's hard to find his way about,
But suddenly he gives a shout.

As Rupert races up the slope he gives a cry of surprise. "There's nobody carrying the Christmas tree. It's moving by itself. It must be a magic one!" Hardly knowing what to do he pauses, while the tree, using its roots for legs, moves rapidly away into the gloom.

Soon Rupert's close enough to see,
There's no one with the Christmas tree!

The chase goes on in the moonlight until some broken rocks are reached. These present no difficulty to the Christmas tree, which uses its roots and branches and climbs easily. When it is at the top it bends backwards towards Rupert and a squeaky voice says, "Go back, go back. You're in danger here."

The tree calls out, "Do not come near!
It's dangerous for you up here."

Rupert struggles up the rocks just as dawn is breaking and as he reaches the top, a little form bars his way and a stern voice bids him stop. It is the keeper of the secret wood! "Gracious, what are you doing here?" pants Rupert.

The keeper stands and bars the way,
He's looking very cross today.

"Now come with me!" the queer man cries.
"A lesson you must learn," he sighs.

"Oh, please don't look so cross," cries Rupert. "There were so many mysteries about the way the Christmas tree came. When it went away again so secretly I just had to follow and find where it was going." The little man frowns again. "No, you didn't have to. There was no need at all," he says heavily.

"Someone ought to teach you a lesson, little bear, and that lesson is: don't be inquisitive." Rupert looks so sorry for himself that the man gradually smiles again. "Come on," he says, "you did me a good turn once. I'll show you the tree."

When Rupert's able to explain,
The keeper starts to smile again.

"All right," he says, "you once helped me.
I'll let you see your Christmas tree."

The odd little man puts the blindfold on Rupert for a short way and then takes it off again. Rupert gasps in surprise. "Look! There's my Christmas tree back in the ground. I know it's my tree because my fairy's still on the top twig. Oh, I do wish you'd tell me how you got to my cottage to dress the tree without anyone hearing you!"

The little man laughs at Rupert's question. "I never came near your cottage," he chuckles. As he stops speaking the tree bends towards the astonished little bear and asks him to help himself to the fairy.

The tree bends down and softly speaks,
"Do take the fairy doll," it squeaks.

RUPERT'S CHRISTMAS TREE

When Rupert has put the Christmas tree fairy in his pocket the blindfold is placed over his eyes for the last time and he is led back through the rocky hill. The little man unties the blindfold and in a flash he has disappeared into the rocks.

The keeper says, "Now run along.
To be so curious is wrong."

Rupert looks round for him in bewilderment and then advances to the entrance to the passage. To his horror the morning is colder and snow is falling heavily. "This is terrible!" he says. "That secret forest was beautifully warm. Now how on earth am I to get home without being completely frozen?"

Poor Rupert sighs to see the snow,
For he has quite a way to go.

He meets his little chums, who stare
To see him in his night clothes there.

When Rupert is halfway home a group of his pals appears over a slope, starting on a sledging party. "Oo, look at Rupert!" shouts Algy Pug. "He's still wearing pyjamas and bedroom slippers. What's your game, Rupert? Where've you been?"

Rupert can tell his pals nothing, except that he must get home at once. Bill is worried to see him in such a state. "We must get him home quickly," he says. Algy wraps his overcoat round the little bear, they sit him on the sledge and set off at full speed for Nutwood.

They wrap him up and rub him too,
Which is the best that they can do.

When Rupert reaches home again,
He's much too cold then to explain.

When the little procession reaches Nutwood, Mrs. Bear is waiting for them. "Good gracious, Rupert, we've been so worried," she cries. "Where have you been?" After a hot bath and with a plate of soup before him Rupert feels none the worse.

Suddenly he pauses and looks at his parents with a mischievous twinkle in his eye. "I've been out learning a lesson," he says. "A lesson? What sort of lesson?" cries Mrs. Bear. "I've got it off by heart," laughs Rupert. "It's just this: DON'T BE INQUISITIVE."

"I've learned my lesson!" Rupert sighs,
"The keeper of the woods is wise."

Rupert and his friends are at a moonlight party in Tigerlily's mysterious garden. Suddenly the little Chinese girl waves her wand and all except Rupert disappear. "Oh dear, they've vanished!" he cries. "Where have they gone?" "They not go; they still here," laughs Tigerlily. (She is quite right. Bill Badger is there, so are Algy Pug, Podgy Pig, Edward Trunk, Willie Whisker, Rex and Reggie Rabbit and Freddy and Ferdy Fox. Also Tigerlily's two cats. Can you see where they all are?)

RUPERT and JACK FROST

Telling how Rupert
attended the meeting
of the Snowmen and
brought home the prizes.

One wintry day, our Rupert waits
For Bill and Edward, his playmates.

It is in the middle of winter and Rupert has arranged an afternoon walk with his two pals, Edward Trunk and Bill Badger. "You're just in time," cries the little bear. "There's going to be a downpour of rain. We'd better shelter indoors for a few minutes."

The wind rises and it gets colder and colder. Then the storm breaks. "Why, it isn't rain, it's a snowstorm," cries Bill. "I do hope it won't melt as soon as it falls." But it keeps on heavily and within a few minutes all the ground is white.

But suddenly it starts to snow,
So for their walk they cannot go.

The chums run out with great delight,
And all join in a grand snow fight.

The snowstorm is only a short one and soon the little pals are able to run out and begin a snow fight. Rupert and Bill take sides against Edward, and in their excitement no one notices the little figure coming down the slope until they are interrupted by a little high-pitched voice.

"Why, it's Lily Duckling!" cries Rupert. Edward asks her to join the snow fight, but she says it would be too rough for her. "Then let's make a snowman," suggests Bill.

When Lily Duckling comes their way,
They ask her if she'd like to play.

Building the snowman is great fun. First the little pals roll a large snowball for the base, then most of the work is done by Edward, who piles snow on it with his large spade. When he stops for a rest Rupert and Bill add their small shovelfuls, while Lily Duckling pats and pushes the 'man' into shape.

"Let's make a snowman now," cries Bill,
And so they set to with a will.

"We'd better make his head soon or he'll be so tall he'll be out of reach," laughs Edward. Rupert glances up. "There's someone else coming," he cries. "I do believe its old Mr. Anteater."

They certainly have lots of fun,
Till soon their task is nearly done.

"Look! Mr. Anteater," they cry,
As their old friend is passing by.

The four pals run and ask their old friend Mr. Anteater to watch them finish their work. To their surprise Mr. Anteater looks as though something is worrying him. Seeing their disappointment Mr. Anteater hurries to praise the little pals.

"You built that snowman jolly well," he says. "But do you think you've made him look quite as nice as you might have done?" He pauses. "Come with me and I'll give you something." Then he leads away the two puzzled little friends.

He says, "That's good, I do declare.
But come with me, young Rupert Bear."

"Take this cigar and old silk hat;
Your snowman will look smart in that!"

When old Mr. Anteater arrives at his own house he explains his curious behaviour. "It's that snowman," he says. "With that cap on his head and twig in his mouth you made him look rather an ordinary sort of person. Wait here and I'll get you something better."

He goes indoors and, to Rupert's astonishment, brings out an old silk hat and a cigar which he hands over. Rupert and Bill run back in great glee to show their new treasures to Edward and Lily Duckling, who at once enter into the fun.

They add a buttonhole and stick,
Then laugh to see their clever trick.

They are so proud of his appearance that they can't bear to leave him until Rupert suddenly hears a distant call. "That means it's teatime," he says. "I'll be back later and I'll bring my mummy and daddy."

They've had great fun they all agree,
But now they must go home for tea.

Rupert is so excited about his afternoon's work that after tea, and while it is still light, Mr. and Mrs. Bear go with him into the snow. "My word," cries Mr. Bear, "he's wonderful! I've never seen such a snowman." But Rupert has caught sight of some curious marks in the white surface.

"There's our fine snowman!" Rupert cries.
His parents stare with great surprise.

Rupert asks if he may stay out a little longer, and when they are gone he looks more closely at the mysterious footmarks. He follows the tracks away from the snowman and finds that they lead towards a tree.

When Rupert's left alone, he sees
Some tiny footprints by the trees.

As Rupert rounds the tree he pulls up with a start, "Good gracious, who are you?" gasps the little bear. "Wait a minute, I've seen you before! Aren't you Jack Frost?" "I'm glad you remember me," grins the boy. "I've just been round to all the snowmen in Nutwood to give them their orders."

The little bear gets quite a fright,
When cheeky Jack Frost pops in sight.

"Whatever do you mean about giving snowmen orders?" cried Rupert. "Can they understand you?" "Ssh! Not so loud," whispers Jack Frost, peering cautiously round the tree. "I really ought not to be seen by anyone, though I don't mind you. If you wait, I'll show you something."

The tiny chap says, "I've been out
To see the snowmen round about."

Seeing the little bear still looking so puzzled, Jack Frost smiles and takes something from his wallet. "You don't like the cold," he says. "Well, here's an Icicle Pill. Just swallow that and see what happens."

He gives the little bear a pill,
And says, "This will prevent a chill."

RUPERT AND JACK FROST

Rupert swallows the Icicle Pill and waits to see if anything happens. Then a strange look comes over his face and he unfastens his overcoat. "Well, how extraordinary!" he says. "It's gone quite warm all of a sudden. I don't believe I need my coat at all!"

"Come on!" cries Jack, "please don't delay.
We must be going right away."

Now it is nearly dark with the moon just rising. "Come on, we'd better start or we shall be late," says Jack suddenly. "Well, I shan't need this heavy overcoat in any case," says Rupert, and folding it up he pops it into a hollow tree.

"I feel so warm," says Rupert Bear;
"I'll leave my overcoat in there."

RUPERT AND JACK FROST

The snowmen come from left and right.
It is a most amazing sight.

Jack Frost leads the way and the two pals run across the crisp snow until they reach a sharp little hill with a flat top. Sure enough some strange, lumpy, white figures are plodding clumsily up the slopes.

"Ha, ha! I thought that would surprise you," laughs Jack. "You're quite right. Those are snowmen from Nutwood!" At that moment a cracked, wheezy voice makes him turn and there is his own snowman. "Ha, Rupert!" he cries, "so you're coming with us? I'm glad."

Then Rupert sees his own snowman
Come plodding up, fast as he can.

He asks him, "Snowman, tell me, do,
Exactly where we're going to?"

As Rupert pours out questions the snowman stops and looks at him kindly. "You really needn't be surprised," he says in his curious, cracked voice. "We snowmen, of course, have to stay very still during the day, but very few people know what we do after dark."

"You're very lucky to be in on this trip. Jack Frost must have taken a great fancy to you. It's a great honour." Rupert stares. "But what is the trip?" he asks. "Where are we going?"

But when he's going to explain,
Jack Frost comes running back again.

RUPERT AND JACK FROST

Says Jack, "It's getting very late.
I fear no longer can we wait."

Before anyone can answer Rupert's questions there is an interruption as Jack Frost marches briskly up to the group. Producing a slender little ice whistle and putting it to his lips he blows a shrill, high note.

Hardly has the whistle blown when there is a strange, deep noise in the distance and suddenly Rupert feels himself lifted and whirled away up among the stars. Then he sees that the others are in the air around him and are not looking at all surprised.

A mighty rushing fills the air,
And whirls away the little bear.

After a few minutes Rupert finds he
is getting used to his extraordinary
journey and is even enjoying it. The
little party sail through the air out of
the darkness and into the curious light.
Over the first of the jagged ice peaks
they go and then the wind begins
to slacken.

They sail across high peaks of ice,
And Rupert finds it is quite nice.

Rupert feels himself falling down until
he drops right into the middle of a
broad, soft snowfield. Ahead of him
is a strange ice palace, and into it Jack
Frost disappears while the others crowd
after him.

He slowly glides down very low,
Then lands quite safely in the snow.

They go inside a palace grand;
It's made of ice, like all this land.

At the top stands Jack Frost. "Well, Rupert," cries the boy, "how did you like that journey?" "It was wonderful," laughs Rupert.

As soon as Jack Frost has seen his party safely inside the palace, he orders the snowmen into single file, and running to the head of them he leads them out into a courtyard and up some more steps on to a terrace. Rupert follows across the shiny, icy courtyard. "They look very business-like now," he thinks. "I wonder if Jack wants me to join the line."

They climb the stairway, led by Jack,
With Rupert keeping at the back.

An angry guard, armed with a spear
Asks Rupert, "What do you want here?"

Up on the higher terrace Rupert is suddenly met by an odd little figure. "Hi, who are you?" demands the little man. "We don't allow strangers here. Come with me."

Feeling very unhappy, Rupert is marched inside the palace and through long ice corridors with barred windows on either side. "Please tell me who you are," he pleads, "and tell me why I can't follow Jack Frost and the snowmen." "I'm one of the guards of the palace," says the fierce little man. "I'm going to lock you up."

The guard takes Rupert to a cell,
Then hurries off, the King to tell.

All at once Rupert hears a voice calling outside. He listens and the voice comes nearer. "I do believe it's someone calling my name!" he cries. Jumping up he runs to the larger window. "Here I am," he shouts. "Who is that?"

When Rupert hears a sudden shout,
He wonders what it's all about.

The next moment the smiling face of Jack Frost appears beyond the bars. "Why didn't you follow me and the snowmen?" he asks. "I did follow you," says Rupert, "but I was too far behind and one of your palace guards took me and locked me up here."

It is Jack Frost, who's come to find,
Why Rupert lags so far behind.

Rupert steps down from the window and listens while there is more calling and shouting outside. Then there is the sound of a key grating in the lock and the next moment Jack Frost appears and leads him out of the cell.

Jack soon releases Rupert Bear,
And tells the guard to take more care.

Leaning over the parapet he points to the courtyard below. "They're waiting for the big moment," says Jack. "You see, every winter I bring the finest snowmen here to be inspected by King Frost. This winter the best I could find were in Nutwood."

"Each year," says Jack, "I have to bring
The finest snowmen to the King."

Rupert manages to run across to his own snowman, who is standing still and looking very proud. "I must see if I can smarten you up at all," he says. "Hi! Come back," shouts Jack. "You're too late. You mustn't touch him again."

So Rupert runs to his snowman,
To make him smarter if he can.

At Jack's cry Rupert obediently goes back and stands beside him. The next moment a remarkable figure appears. He has a spiky crown and an ermine collar, and the end of his long robe is held up by a train-bearer. "It must be the King! How fine he looks," whispers Rupert.

The King appears, so tall and grand;
A sparkling wand held in his hand.

The little bear with pleasure sighs
When his own snowman wins the prize.

In the silence everyone stands very quiet, wondering what will happen next. Then the King seems to make up his mind. He calls Rupert's own snowman to come forward. The proud, white figure steps out of the line, and the King hangs a lovely jewel round his neck.

"I give you this because you are the best snowman of the winter," he says. When the excitement has died down the King looks at Rupert. "It isn't often we have strangers here," he says. "I've been wondering who you were."

The King then turns to Rupert Bear,
And asks him what he's doing there.

"Now come with me!" commands the King,
And Rupert follows wondering.

King Frost praises Rupert for his excellent work until the little bear feels very shy, although he is so proud. "This is all very exciting," thinks Rupert. "I do wonder what's going to happen now."

The procession enters the tower and while the guard stops outside a door the King leads the way into a private apartment, while Jack Frost and Rupert follow. At one side of the room is an ornamental board and fastened to it are lots of brilliant medals, stars and brooches.

They stand before some gleaming boards,
On which are pinned the King's awards.

Leaving the small, private apartment, King Frost goes into a great hall and takes his seat on a royal throne, with guards on either side. Then he gives the bright star to Jack, and the boy pins it on Rupert's chest. "This is a special prize for you," he says, "because you have made one of the best snowmen who has ever come here."

Then to the little bear's delight,
Jack Frost gives him a medal bright.

Jack Frost leads Rupert away, but very soon a guard runs after them. He holds out three papers to the little bear. "These are from King Frost," he says.

A guard runs out and cries, "I bring
These invitations from the King."

It's time to leave this land of snow,
So to the palace tower they go.

Then Jack Frost leads him outside. Ahead of them is a tall tower with a flat top, and some of the party have already assembled there, including his own snowman. The King bids them farewell from a window.

Entering the tower, Rupert and Jack Frost climb up to the flat top, where all the Nutwood snowmen are already assembled. At that instant there is the clang of a bell from a nearby tower, and all eyes turn in that direction. Then a figure leans from the bell tower with a warning shout.

Just then they hear a warning cry
Come from the bell-tower just nearby.

*A bird from Nutwood comes to say
That there the snow has gone away.*

While all the snowmen and Rupert gaze, they notice a speck in the sky. It is a great bird, which swoops towards them and swirls about their heads. "I have a message for His Majesty. He must have it at once," squawks the bird.

Jack Frost takes Rupert on to a platform and at once the King joins them. "My faithful messenger reports that warm weather has reached Nutwood," he says. "Therefore I decree that these five snowmen shall not go back, but shall stay with me until next winter."

*Then King Frost says, "Well now I fear,
The Nutwood snowmen must stay here."*

"I cannot stay here!" Rupert cries.
"We'll see the King," Jack Frost replies.

"Please let me go back," Rupert says. "My mummy and daddy would get terribly worried if I stayed away all that time." Seeing that Rupert will not remain with him, Jack Frost rather sorrowfully takes him on to the terrace.

"Rupert thinks he must return to Nutwood," says Jack. "Will Your Majesty permit me to summon a special wind to take him back!" "The little bear is our honoured guest," says the King. "He may do just what he pleases. He shall return to his home."

To their surprise the King agrees,
And says, "You may do as you please."

Before he goes, the little bear
Collects the things the snowmen wear.

Before starting home Rupert has another idea. "All those hats and things that make the snowmen look so fine belong to my pals," he says. "Do you think I could take them back with me?" "Of course you can," cries Jack.

In a moment Rupert is beginning to collect the things. When all is ready, Jack Frost gives Rupert his instructions. "I must stay and see that the snowmen start their work," says the boy. "So you must go alone. Now go to the tower again, but wait until I give you the signal."

Says Jack, "I cannot come with you,
But I will tell you what to do."

Saying goodbye to Jack Frost, Rupert then carries the sack up to the tower. Suddenly the great bell swings with a loud clang. "Now for it!" he thinks. Then he blows the whistle.

So Rupert says goodbye once more,
And hears the bell that rang before.

Hardly has the sound of the whistle died away when again comes a distant rumble, and the next instant a giant wind has caught Rupert and whirled him off the tower, over the ice mountains, and up among the stars. "I do hope I'm going in the right direction," he gasps, as the aurora lights fade behind him.

The wind returns with all its power,
And whirls poor Rupert from the tower.

RUPERT AND JACK FROST

*To his relief, he finds that he
Has landed safely in a tree.*

Rupert realises that he is going more
slowly and dropping towards the Earth.
Nearer and nearer he falls. Then
suddenly he is caught by the thick,
yielding outer branches of a tree. In his
surprise he drops the stick and sack and
grabs to save himself as he slithers
through the lower branches.

When he gets his breath back Rupert
unhitches the sack and the stick from
the branches and drops them to the
ground. Then he gives a shout. "Why
this is the very tree where I found Jack
Frost!" he cries.

*"Well this is strange!" gasps Rupert Bear.
"I wonder if my coat is there?"*

He finds his coat and hurries back,
Still carrying his precious sack.

Leaving the stick in the stand he bursts into the living room, where his parents gaze at him in astonishment. While he has his supper Rupert tries to tell his parents about his wonderful journey, but it all sounds so odd that they don't know what to make of it. "You must have been dreaming," says Mrs. Bear.

As he goes to bed he gets an idea. "The lovely star that King Frost gave me," he cries. He glances down, but to his dismay there is nothing left but a little damp place on his jersey.

Then Rupert has a big surprise,
"My lovely star has gone!" he cries.

Next day, his chums call round to say
The snowmen have all gone away.

The next morning there is a great clamour outside his cottage, and opening the door he finds lots of his pals gathered there. "All the snowmen in Nutwood have vanished," says Bill, "but, what's more extraordinary, all their hats and things have gone too!"

To their surprise, Rupert only chuckles. "It's been a wonderful story, and I wish some of you had been with me." Just then a familiar figure appears and Rupert breaks into a trot. "Come on," he says. "I want Mr. Anteater to hear it first."

They meet their kind old friend again,
And Rupert hurries to explain.

As the pals run up to him, Mr. Anteater greets them. "Hullo, Rupert," he says. "I was just going to see your snowman, but I can't find him." Rupert smiles. "Thanks to your hat and cigar, he became the finest snowman of the winter," he cries. "King Frost gave him first prize." The old gentleman stares. "I can't understand a word of that," he grumbles.

But Rupert's story sounds so tall,
They cannot quite believe it all.

Finally, amid much excitement, Rupert gives to Bill and Edward and Lily Duckling the invitations for them to go and visit King Frost.

Cries Rupert, "This will prove it true.
These invitations are for you."

RUPERT

THE **DAILY EXPRESS** ANNUAL

BIBLIOGRAPHY

STORIES

Listed chronologically

'Rupert and the Tiny Flute', *Rupert in More Adventures* Annual, 1944, pp. 32–42.

'Rupert's Rainy Adventure', *Rupert in More Adventures* Annual, 1944, pp. 92–100.

'Rupert's Christmas Tree', *More Adventures of Rupert* Annual, 1947, pp. 107–118.

'Rupert and Jack Frost', *The Rupert Book* Annual, 1948, pp. 5–20.

'Rupert and Ninky', *Rupert* Annual, 1949, pp. 5–19.

'Rupert and the Mare's Nest', *More Rupert Adventures* Annual, 1952, pp. 5–29.

'Rupert and the Lost Cuckoo', *Rupert* Annual, 1963, pp. 44–62.

'Rupert and Raggety', *Rupert* Annual, 1969, pp. 72–92.

PUZZLES

Listed in order of appearance

Page 68, 'Rupert and the Bs', activity, *More Rupert Adventures* Annual, 1952, p. 119.

Page 120, 'Rupert's Short Cut', activity, *Rupert in More Adventures* Annual, 1944, p. 2.

Page 234, 'Tigerlily's Party', activity, *Rupert in More Adventures* Annual, 1944, p. 119.

ENDPAPERS

Listed in order of appearance

Pages 22–23, 'Autumn Elf and the Imps in the Pine Trees, endpaper, *Rupert* Annual, 1957.

Pages 66–67, 'Little Chinese Islands', endpaper, *Rupert* Annual, 1969.

Pages 118–119, 'King of the Birds', endpaper, *More Rupert Adventures* Annual, 1952.

Pages 158–159, 'Hovercraft', endpaper, *Rupert* Annual, 1968.

Pages 208–209, 'Frog Chorus', endpaper, *Rupert* Annual, 1958.

Pages 266–267, 'Night – Santa Claus', endpaper, *The New Rupert Book* Annual, 1951.

COVERS

Listed in order of appearance

Page xviii, 'Rupert and Friends Overlooking the Sea', cover, *Rupert in More Adventures* Annual, 1944.

Page 24, 'Rupert and the Fish on its Tail', cover, *Rupert* Annual, 1969.

Page 160, 'Rupert and the Merboy', cover, *Rupert* Annual, 1963.

Page 178, 'Christmas Carol Singers', cover, *Rupert* Annual, 1949.

Page 210, 'Rupert on a Sledge', cover, *The Rupert Book* Annual, 1956.

Page 268, 'Rupert in a Flying Saucer', cover, *Rupert* Annual, 1966.